Adventure House
Presents

MARVEL TALES

December 1939

This reprint edition is a facsmile edition. Variations in print
and quality are mostly attributable to the rough woodpulp
original this reprint edition is based on.

ISBN: 1-59798-059-5

Published by Adventure House
914 Laredo Road
Silver Spring, Md 20901
www.adventurehouse.com
sales@adventurehouse.com

Vol. 1 No. 6 December, 1939

FOR MORE GRIPPING STORIES READ THE CURRENT ISSUES OF:

UNCANNY TALES AND **MYSTERY TALES**

NEW ISSUES NOW ON SALE!

MARVEL TALES published every-other-month by Western Fiction Pub. Co., Inc. Office of publication 4600 Diversey Ave., Chicago, Ill. Entered as second class matter April 25, 1938, at the Post Office at Chicago, Ill., under Act of March 3, 1879. Editorial and Executive offices, 330 W. 42nd St., McGraw-Hill Bldg., New York, N. Y. Yearly subscription, 90 cents. Not responsible for unsolicited scripts.

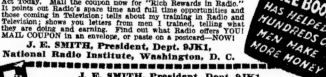

THE ANGEL

BY NILS O. SONDERLUND

*Author of "Satan's
Legion of the
Damned," etc.*

CHAPTER I

THE FREEZING MUSIC

His boot came down savagely

THE piping was a thin cold sound. Like a flight of crystal arrows, the high notes of it reached Carter Boyd's racing plane. Its eerie chill sent a shudder down his hard, air-trained body.

He knew that it wasn't really sound at all. He was a full mile above this bleak North-China desert, five from the strange dog-fight ahead. The six

AMAZING BOOK-LENGTH NOVEL OF A LUST-MAD EARTH-MAN HORDE

FROM HELL

Could this hell-spawned golden bird-girl dispel at last the shadow of ageless tragedy from Carter Boyd's earth-man heart? And had his passionate love for her made civilization's doom a horrible certainty, and delivered ten million mortals into the hands of the Alexander's Gray Minions and their ghastly G-Ray?

With a last prodigious effort Hall dragged himself up against the appalling pressure

hundred horsepower of the Russian-built motor was bellowing before him. He couldn't have heard a shout at his ear.

Yet that mysterious piping came clear and flawless to him, as if he had heard it in a still moonlit garden, with some nude spring-goddess dancing to its weird, disturbing melody. Somehow, it set an uncanny picture in his mind.

Carter Boyd wasn't the type that is given to visions. He was a lean, hard-headed young American. His thin face carried a perpetual whimsical grin. His dark eyes, however, were apt to show a solemn reflection of the flying accident that had shattered his life.

The fault was a rookie pilot's, not his own. But four lives were blanked out, three of which he counted the most precious in the world. Boyd's

THAT PITTED SUPER-SCIENCE AGAINST ETERNITY'S GOLDEN BIRD-GIRL!

hair, within six months, had turned completely white. It was a year before his hands were steady enough to fly again. Then he had come to China.

In a year and a half, he had earned a number of medals and several thousand dollars—which he had turned back into a relief fund for refugee children. Now one of the most trusted officers in the Chinese service, he had been sent to investigate reports of strange planes operating above the Gobi.

That desert lay beneath him now. The vastest and most hostile of the world's unconquered wildernesses. Farther than his mind could reach, it spread waterless wastes of yellow drifting dunes, treeless cragged mountains, arid canyon-chopped bad lands.

Somewhere behind him, on the ancient caravan trail that now was rutted with the wheels of trucks, was a supply depot. A skipping beat in the motor had worried him. He had been wondering what would happen if he never got back. Between hunger and thirst and the Mongol nomads, it wouldn't be anything very pleasant.

Carter Boyd forgot all danger, however, when he saw the dog-fight ahead. Three planes were attacking a fourth. There was something queer about the fourth plane. It seemed, for one thing, oddly small. Wheeling, rolling, sideslipping, it was evading the others with a matchless skill. But still the three were forcing it slowly down, toward the red wind-carved teeth of the wilderness.

Boyd was puzzled. He studied the gray attackers, through his binoculars. They were neither Japanese, he thought, nor Russian. Something was radically novel about their design. The taper of their wings suggested some great bird. Unfamiliar ailerons heightened the likeness. Here were aerodynamic principles, Boyd thought, that

were unknown to western designers.

But the fourth plane was stranger still.

It was a monoplane, too. But if the attackers seemed birdlike, it looked like an actual bird! Boyd couldn't quite understand what he saw. He thought those bright-colored wings really rose and fell—

Then he heard that thin cold piping.

He shuddered to the eldritch chill of it, as if every piercing crystal note had been an ice-cold blade. And it did something else to him, something beyond comprehension.

For a moment it blotted out the bleak red maze of sandstone canyons a mile beneath him. It hid the specks of the four planes ahead, dancing insect-like in that puzzling engagement. And he saw an eerie being.

A winged woman!

Or was she woman?

She was soaring toward him, on powerful slender pinions that were feathered like some mighty bird's. Pure silver lined them. They were tipped and covered gorgeously, with flaming purple and delicate mauve and subtle hints of green.

HER face was a woman's. Beneath a close-fitting scarlet helmet, it was pointed, elfin, golden. The small mouth was a burning red, tense with distress.

Her body was a woman's, too. The sweet curves of it were shining with a yellow velvet down. The breasts were firm round golden bowls, quivering to the effort of her wings.

She was piping, as she soared. The pipe was a long silver tube, oddly keyed and knobbed. She held it with her feet—which, really, he saw, were delicate golden hands. Tiny yellow fingers formed the exotic rhythm of that maddening music.

Carter Boyd felt his heart pump

faster. Those full lips moved, and he read their scarlet promise. He looked into the deep pools of her eyes, dark with pain and desire. And he wanted her.

But she couldn't be! His reason made outraged protest. There were beautiful women. There were birds that soared with a matchless grace. But there could be no being who mingled the beauty of woman and bird—

Boyd caught his breath. A flaming eagerness stilled that voice of reason. He forgot all her strangeness, and saw only the things that made her woman, the golden breasts and haunting eyes, the alluring contours and the scarlet mouth.

The eerie minors of her piping music called to him. He heard the mating-songs of birds, and felt the throbbing heart of all earth's spring. The music was challenge and question and promise. He wanted to reach out and take her. He thirsted for the feel of her golden body in his arms, and the contact of her lips. He made a groping movement toward her — and a queer cold froze him.

That cold was as uncanny, as sourceless, as her music. It came from nowhere, through the cockpit and through his heavy flying suit. It ached in his bones and stiffened his body. And the red full lips, against that golden elfish face, curved into a mocking smile.

Distantly, as if it had been miles from him, Carter Boyd sensed the sputter of his motor. An urgent sense of danger shook him. And that eerie music ended, as abruptly as it had begun.

The cold ebbed away, and Carter Boyd was back in his pursuit plane. His unconsciously tensed muscles had pulled it into a steep climb, and the motor was missing alarmingly. He pushed the stick hastily forward.

He was still shivering. That deadly cold had been actual, and no illusion. The wings and gun and cockpit cowling were gleaming with white frost. The motor was cold; he dived, gunned it.

Questions hammered at Carter Boyd's brain. Who was that bright-winged golden bird-woman? And where? What was the secret of her uncanny, soundless piping? And whence had come that deadly cold?

Danger thrust away those questions. For the plane had hurtled on, through the vision. The four planes wheeling in that puzzling dog fight were nearer, now. And one of the three gray attackers abruptly left the pursuit, and climbed toward him.

Carter Boyd tipped the pursuit ship into a long dive, to meet the strange machine. He gunned the motor again, and saw a spatter of fine black drops across the windshield. Something wrong with an oil line—

But he forgot that peril, staring at another of the gray machines, that had dived upon the tiny, fleeing plane. For the gray ship turned abruptly white. It failed to come out of the dive, and went plunging down past the little plane, and made a dark little burst of smoke against a sandstone cliff.

Carter Boyd shuddered. It was that same weird cold, he knew, that silvered the gray plane with frost, and stiffened its occupants, and sent them to death against the cliff. He wondered if those unknown men had seen the bird-woman, and heard her eerie piping.

But the approaching stranger was now within range of him. Synchronized guns on its forward cockpit began spitting through the propeller. That was all the invitation that Carter Boyd required.

REGARDLESS of the increasing spray of oil on the windshield, he hammered the throttle of his motor wide open, and plunged to meet the attack. He had been hired to defend China from aerial invasion, and he wasn't going to shirk the job. Air combat was a deadly game that gripped him with the same utter fascination that some men find in cards or ticker tape or horses or women. It was what made life liveable.

He fired a trial burst, to warm his own twin guns. With a blinding speed, however, the attacker was already upon him. Bullets ripped into his right wing. He slipped off to the left, seeking to avoid that deadly hail. Rolling, he tried to come up under the belly of the other ship.

With a dazzling, incredible speed, the gray machine banked and turned back upon him. Boyd just had time to glimpse the emblem painted on its slender fuselage — the representation of a rough black rock, spreading black wings beneath a yellow crown.

That ensign was neither Japanese nor Chinese nor Russian. But Boyd didn't have long to wonder about it. For the man in the rear cockpit swung his swivel mounted guns over the side, and tracer bullets made white streaks.

Bullets smashed into Boyd's wings. This was a better fighting ship, he knew, than he had ever met before. And its crew, whoever they were, knew their stuff.

It was a reckless Immelman turn, executed with every inch of that added speed for which the Russian designers of his plane had traded safety, that brought him up under the gray plane's belly at last.

The other pilot side-slipped, rolled. Boyd clung to his position, desperately. His hammering guns whipped fragments from the gray machine.

Suddenly, in the middle of an attempted loop, the gray ship fell off on one wing. A black plume of smoke trailed out behind it. Boyd saw the limp form of the gunner, hanging half out of his cockpit.

Boyd leveled his own plane. The increasing smear of oil on the windshield blinded him. He lifted himself into the windstream, to clean it with a piece of waste, and his nostrils caught the reek of raw gasoline. He saw white drops trailing back from one of the wing tanks — and knew that now he would never get back to the depot.

And still the battle wasn't done. He saw that tiny, bright-winged ship forced down upon a tiny, ragged scrap of mesa. His breath caught with pity for the unknown pilot. But the little ship checked itself, landed safely. Its strange wings seemed somehow to fold. And the other gray attacker lifted toward Boyd.

He gunned his motor, banked to meet it. Its forward guns hammered lead at him. He waved swiftly back and forth, firing. He meant to dive at the last instant, to seek that same blind spot that had doomed the other plane.

But smoking oil covered the windshield. When he peered above, it sprayed his goggles and burned his face. The other plane was lost in a blur of gray.

The indicator showed falling oil pressure, and Boyd's motor was developing a bad heat-knock. Its power was failing. At the crucial instant of the loop, when he was hanging on the prop, it failed to deliver the vital thrust.

In that lost instant, the gray plane banked above him. Its rear guns spat merciless lead. A cold shock struck Boyd's shoulder. In the first instant, he hardly felt it. But a dull ache increased, and he felt the hot stickiness of blood.

Boyd had been hit before. He knew that this was just about the finish. But he opened the throttle all the way, climbing. Thundering in that last effort, the motor threw out a black cloud of smoke and oil. The oil pressure had dropped to zero. There were only a few seconds left, but Boyd grimly set himself to use them.

He tore off his goggles. Burning oil stung his eyes. The motor stopped, hot pistons frozen. But, from an outside loop that looked like the beginning of a helpless spin, Boyd flung his smoking ship into the gray machine's flank.

Caught napping, the other gunner tried to answer his fire. But Boyd's sights crossed his body, and it flopped grotesquely back. Then, because his eyes were filled with oil and tears, Boyd couldn't see anything more.

BLINKING his blinded eyes, he pumped down the landing gear. The pain in his shoulder was growing swiftly keener. Blood soaked down his sleeve. His arm still worked, so he knew no bones were crushed. But loss of blood had made him faint.

At last he could see a little. He found the tiny gravel plateau where the strange little plane had landed. It seemed to be gone, now, or perhaps his streaming eyes just couldn't make it out.

He banked and turned over the dark rugged canyon beyond. Gliding back, he lost flying speed, pancaked on the rim. The shock sent a blinding sickness of pain over all Boyd's body.

The landing gear collapsed, and a great boulder crumpled a wing. The next thing Boyd knew, he was lying on the gravel a dozen yards away. He heard the explosive *puff* when the gasoline ignited, and made a faint effort to move.

He failed. His wounded arm was useless. He was stunned, groggy with concussion. Dimly, he knew that the exploding tanks would get him. But there wasn't anything that he could do about it.

Lying there, waiting for that searing spray of exploding gasoline, Carter Boyd thought he had probably twenty seconds to live. And then he wondered if his estimate hadn't been twenty seconds in error. For he saw an angel.

A shadow passed over the sun. He blinked his smarting eyes, tried to raise his head. Bright wings wheeled above him, like the wings of the strange tiny ship he had sought to aid.

Only it wasn't a plane. It was the winged bird-woman, whose uncanny piping he had heard in that singular vision. The sun shimmered on the velvet rounds of her golden breasts. Silver-lined wings folded slightly, and she dropped toward him.

Red lips were provocatively parted, in her elfin yellow face. She made a soft cooing sound—and that was lost in the crackle of flame. Boyd saw racing blue tongues reach the gasoline tank. His helpless body tensed itself against the blast of flaming death.

CHAPTER II

GOAL UNKNOWN

SOMETHING happened the instant that Jimmy Hall saw Linda Gaylord. Her red hair stood out like a torch from the group crowding aboard the big pilot's transport, and a gust of lake breeze momentarily molded blue silk against her slim, full-breasted body.

And it happened. She was one of those few women, Jimmy Hall knew, so utterly beautiful that clothing is an outrage to their loveliness. Eagerly, his blue eyes stripped the clinging silk from her exquisite white form—and he knew that she sensed all the meaning of his look.

Her gray eyes met his for a moment,

alertly quizzical. The mocking hint of a smile on her full scarlet lips seemed to challenge: *I dare you!*

Then her wolfish escort seized her slim white arm possessively, and swept her away from him. But already the damage was done. As Jimmy Hall gunned the big silver transport into a stiff lake breeze, for the Chicago-Kansas City run, he found it very difficult to get that mop of red hair out of his mind.

It was the sort of mahogany-and-flame hair that made him long to tangle his fingers in it. Something in the girl's level gray eyes had warned him to expect difficulties about that. But Jimmy Hall thought it would be worth a good deal of trouble.

He found out Linda's name from the stewardess. Presently, while his co-pilot took the controls, he walked back down the aisle. He even stopped at Linda's seat, to point out the broad silver curves of the Mississippi, beneath.

She smiled back at him, with a dazzle that caught his breath. A few freckles showed that she was used to wind and sun. Her cheeks dimpled unexpectedly. Perhaps, he hoped, the level look in her gray eyes wasn't going to be an insurmountable barrier, after all.

He noticed that the other passengers were turning to watch him — and decided that he didn't care a bit.

But the man beside Linda did.

Her companion, sitting next to the window, had an arrogant military erectness. His lean, pale, supercilious face had the hungry bitterness of exile. His oil-sleeked hair was very black. He looked—well, wolfish.

His book closed with a bang. His narrowed eyes looked angrily up at Hall. They had, he noticed, a greenish color that he didn't like. The man's sharp, impatient voice had a hissing accent:

"What ees it?"

Jimmy Hall said, flatly, "The Mississippi."

The pale man showed no interest in the Father of waters. He waited, visibly, for Hall to add *sir*—which the big flier neglected to do. The green eyes glanced possessively at Linda Gaylord's loveliness, then lifted again, hard with annoyance.

"We are occupied," he said sharply. "Can't you see?"

Jimmy Hall felt a sudden and almost overpowering desire to poke the pale man's thinly arrogant nose. Beneath Hall's yellow thatch, there were six feet and nearly two hundred pounds of him. His blue eyes blazed a warning, and the stranger drew back uneasily.

But Linda Gaylord smiled her dimpled, dazzling smile again. The mellow soft huskiness of her voice soothed Hall's feelings:

"Sorry, pilot."

Jimmy Hall believed her. He went back forward, and called the stewardess. The tall military man, she told him, was down on the passenger list as Mr. Smithson Jones.

"That's a phony!" he muttered. "Jones! He looks like something they kicked out of the middle of Europe, because they didn't like his manners."

A few minutes later, the radio warned him of a line squall developing unexpectedly ahead. For half an hour, in boiling clouds that blazed with lightning, he fought wind and hail. At last, when the big plane drummed into calm sunlight beyond:

"A nice piece of airmanship, Jim," the co-pilot approved.

And the stewardess came with a message:

"Your red-haired lady wants to speak to you, Jimmy."

WITH his heart skipping eagerly, Hall went back. Mr. Smithson

Jones was reading a book on air-combat. He didn't look up. Linda Gaylord greeted Hall with the same heart-stopping smile.

"Thanks, pilot." Her voice was a husky caress. "A pretty bit of flying. I wanted to ask you to have dinner with us tonight." Hall's smile faded a little when she added, "To discuss a matter of business."

Jimmy Hall had a standing date, on Wednesday nights, to play poker with the gang. But he never thought of that. He agreed instantly, and the girl gave him the address of a Chinese restaurant in Kansas City.

"At nine, Mr. Hall."

At ten o'clock, when he entered Wong Foo's, the red glare of neon gave Smithson Jones a sickly pallor, and his green eyes glittered unpleasantly. But Linda Gaylord, her hair a ruddy flame above clinging silver lame, was excitingly beautiful.

"So sorry we're late."

Jimmy Hall forgave her. He took the cold lax hand of Mr. Jones, who scowled at him, sniffed disgustedly at the smell of cooking in the air, and frowned at a spot on the tablecloth.

Hall had been eager for the meeting. Now he found himself just as eager to end it, for there was something about Mr. Jones that he simply couldn't endure. With one word of soft Cantonese, he sent the fat waiter scurrying, and said:

"Well?"

With a pleasing, candid smile, Linda said immediately:

"Mr. Jones is an agent of Chiang Kai-shek's government. He needs American pilots and instructors. Since you already speak Chinese, Mr. Hall, we can offer you a thousand American dollars a month, to go to China. Will you sign a contract?"

Mr. Jones himself looked distressed at that abrupt statement.

"Secrecy ees essential." His lowered, hissing voice sounded almost fearful. "Speak no word of this, pilot. Here ees the contract."

His pale, claw-like fingers produced the document. Hall scanned it, drumming on the tablecloth. The green feral eyes of Mr. Jones shot a sharp, questioning look at the girl. They both waited, silently. After half a minute, Hall looked up.

"Generous enough," he said. "And I've thought for a long time that the Chinese weren't getting a square deal. I'll sign it."

In the rear of a Chinese curio shop, they found a notary who witnessed the contract. On the street outside, Linda Gaylord handed Jimmy Hall a railroad ticket to a small village in the Rockies, and told him to ask for Lee Carmody.

A sharp disappointment stabbed Hall. Half his reason for signing up had been the desire to see more of Linda. "I hope——" he gulped, "hope we'll be meeting again."

The green eyes of Mr. Jones glittered unpleasantly. The pale claws of his fingers seized the girl's bare white arm, and drew her away.

Lee Carmody was an immense dark man, sitting in his truck beside a freight siding near the mountain village. He waited for sweating men to load the truck with heavy wooden boxes from a car on the siding. Then, with Hall in the cab, the truck rumbled up a narrow road through the pines. Carmody refused to answer any questions.

At last, in the gray chill of an overcast mountain dusk, the truck came out upon a level mountain meadow. Hangars, shops, and barracks nestled against the forest. Gray-clad men stood guard with rifles.

"Guess ye can look around, stranger," Carmody muttered. "Don't try to leave camp. The Boss will be back in the morning."

Hall looked around. What he saw alarmed him. He knew that smuggling war materials out of the United States was a grave offense. And it looked as if his new employer was involved in that.

He saw men in gray unloading the truck. Some of the boxes contained machine guns, rifles, and ammunition, but most of them, he saw, held airplane parts. He glimpsed a huge gray bombing plane, standing in the hangar.

An amazing plane! Hall's trained eyes picked out a dozen new wrinkles in design. Here was a ship, he knew, with the speed and range to carry a load of bombs half around the world. From the jigs and tools in sight, he knew it had been assembled here. Hall hunted up Carmody, and demanded:

"Do you people expect me to fly that job to China?"

"Mister," the big man drawled, "there are three rules you have got to follow, if you want to work for the Trust. Don't ask questions. Don't answer questions. Just obey orders."

Hall slept in the barracks. At dawn, Carmody woke him. Outside, a small monoplane taxied in across the silver-frosted meadow. A slim figure in tan sport skirt and form-fitting crimson sweater leapt out of it. Hall's heart skipped a beat when he saw that it was Linda Gaylord.

HALL followed Carmody to meet her. Her red hair was pushed out of sight under a leather helmet. The close-fitting sweater betrayed the sweet curves of her, the proud up-tilted cups of her breasts.

Hall caught his breath and looked away, to hide the quick pain of his desire. She handed Carmody a gray envelope, and told him briskly:

"The Boss is taking the ship from Base Two. Mr. Hall, here, is going to take off at dusk. I will fly with him. These are your orders."

With her dimpled, dazzling smile, she turned to Hall.

"Breakfast?" she said. "We've got a few things to discuss."

"Okay," Hall said. "I've got several questions, myself."

"Forget them." Her voice was crisply impersonal. "It is your business, Mr. Hall, to obey the instructions that are given you—and forget everything else."

The curt toss of her head infuriated Hall. He was filled with a secret desire to get his hands on her white lovely body, and shake a little of the icy efficiency out of her. A sound spanking, he felt, would put their relations on a much better footing.

He couldn't, however, help feeling a little sorry for her. She looked too pretty and innocent to be mixed up with anything so rotten as this business was beginning to appear. Her quick smile warmed him to the heart.

At breakfast, she told him that they were to take off at dusk for a Chinese airport in Shensi province, beyond Sian. The State Department, she assured Hall, unofficially approved the activities of Mr. Jones. The secrecy was because of Japanese spies.

A bright shaft of the sunrise caught her hair, as she talked, and turned it into red glory. Her beauty caught Hall's breath — and burned away his doubts.

"This still looks fishy, somehow," he thought. "But, darling, I'd fly with you to hell!"

Hall watched the fueling of the big gray bomber, and tested it on a taxi run up and down the long meadow. Working with the girl, he plotted a great-circle course across the Pacific. At dusk they climbed into the plane, but Linda told him to wait.

She watched the starry sky, until the

lights of another plane wheeled above. With phones on her ears, she talked into a microphone, and at last signalled Hall to take off.

"Forget the course we plotted," she said when they were in the air. "Just follow the other ship."

Jimmy Hall wasn't much surprised, but his lean jaw set stubbornly.

"I was hired to fly this ship to China," he said. "I'm going to do it." His blue eyes blazed. "I'll tell you right now, Miss Gaylord, if you wanted a stooge to use in some sort of piratical monkey-business—well, you've got the wrong man!"

"Better obey!" Above the muffled drum of four great motors, the girl's voice was brisk and cold. "Mr. Jones is aboard the other plane. He has a full gun crew, and plenty of ammunition. And this plane isn't armed. He will shoot you down."

"Oh yeah?" Hall grinned at her. "We'll see!"

"Follow the plane!" Her voice had an icy rap. Her blue eyes flashed, and Hall saw the gleam of a little automatic in her hands. "You're in too far to go back now."

Jimmy Hall laughed, happily.

"Linda, darling," he said softly, "I see that I'm going to have to give you a lesson. I'm going to take that little toy away from you. And then I'm going to put you across my lap and turn up your skirt and spank you where it will do the most good."

And he reached out toward her tense, trembling body.

"No you won't!" She turned in the seat, shouting back into the dark cabin space that had been fitted for the use of navigator and commanding officer. "Will he, Krošeć?"

"*Nein!*" boomed a great rusty voice, behind Hall. "Yankee *Schweinhund*, you had better obey. In der name of der Alexander, *Ja!*"

A GUN'S hard muzzle jabbed against Hall's spine. He drew back his reaching hand, and looked at Linda Gaylord. She lowered the little automatic to her lap. Her provocative lips smiled at him, mockingly. Her white hand caressed the full curve of her breasts, with a triumphant, preening gesture.

"Oh yeah, Mr. Hall?" her soft voice jeered. "Now you're working for the Trust," she said more gravely. "Forget the Chinese. Forget everything but your orders. And follow Mr. Jones."

CHAPTER III

WINGED WOMAN

LYING beside his flaming plane, on that tiny gravel plateau in the Gobi, Carter Boyd blinked his dimming eyes. For the bright-winged creature dropping beside him looked more like an angel than most things a gravely wounded airman can expect to see.

Beating through the pall of smoke, her great wings were silver-lined, gorgeous with color. Golden-bodied, golden-breasted, red-crowned and scarlet-lipped, she was weirdly beautiful—and altogether incredible.

Waiting for the explosion, for the deadly spray of burning gasoline, Boyd closed his stinging eyes. He knew that she was a dream of death. He knew that she would be gone when he opened them.

But she wasn't. The great brilliant wings, half-folded, were dropping her perilously close to the flames. All the pain in his battered body, the cold throb of the bullet wound in his shoulder, vanished before a breathless wonder.

He was still alive—with perhaps a

couple of seconds to go. And she was no angel. For angels, whatever they were like, certainly wouldn't possess her remarkable brand of flaming beauty —not if there was to be any order in heaven.

She was almost at his side. He saw her face, beneath the close-fitting scarlet helmet. It was golden, like the rich-curved velvet of her body, but soft-skinned, devoid of the yellow down. Narrow, elfin, it was still completely human. And it was drawn, now, with a desperate concern.

For a gust of wind carried a rippling banner of yellow flame between them. Boyd's helpless body quivered beneath a merciless heat. And the bright wings beat desperately away from the licking, avid flames.

Carter Boyd closed his eyes again, to wait for the finish.

And again he heard that eerie, soundless piping. The soundless minor notes of it showered upon him like crystal javelins of cold. His skin prickled and shivered. Cold seared his lungs, ached in his bones. And the crackle and roar of the flames suddenly ended.

With an effort, he opened his stiff eyelids. Frost was crackling on his garments, and on the stones about him. Glittering flakes of ice were dancing in the air. And he saw the bird-woman, piping.

She was just as he had seen her in that puzzling vision. Mighty wings supported her. And the feet at the ends of her shapely golden limbs, that were really tiny graceful hands, were playing that long queer-looking silver pipe.

The piping was not sound. It was some uncanny vibration, that stabbed straight into the brain. It was radiant cold. Boyd shuddered to its eerie chill. He heard the crackle of bitter frost in the air. He saw the last yellow tongue flicker and vanish above the smoking wreckage.

Her piping had extinguished the fire!

Boyd couldn't quite believe that. The sensations of his dimming mind were becoming oddly dream-like. He saw her dropping again, close to him. He watched her tiny golden sharp-nailed hands, telescoping the pipe and snapping it to a shoulder strap.

Then he thought that the fire was bursting up again, but he was beyond alarm. He thought that she had seized his clothing, was lifting him. He knew it must be only a dream. Perhaps this was the last unconscious. Perhaps, after all, she had been a real angel. If so, heaven would be rather more interesting than he had ever expected.

He heard the explosion. But it was only a dull, muffled boom, very far off. He felt no splash of liquid fire. There was only darkness.

Carter Boyd awoke in the frosty silence of dawn. The sky was turning gray beyond black fantastic mountain ramparts, eastward. The desert stars were fading, and a high cloud burst into golden flame.

Awareness of his body returned unpleasantly. His shoulder throbbed to a slow dull ache. His first effort to move stabbed his chest with sharp pain. He lay still, and began fumbling about with his good hand.

He was lying, he found, on a bank of loose dry sand. He felt his stiff, throbbing shoulder. It had been bound up. Probably with his own shirt, for that was missing.

And a queer thing covered him. It had protected him from the chill of the desert night. His fingers explored it. Velvet down lined it. The thin edge of it was stiff and yet yielding. It felt amazingly like a feathered wing.

THAT discovery made him forget the aching stiffness of his body. He turned his head. His breath stopped, and a queer little ache throbbed in his throat. For here, lying beside him on the sand, was—

The angel!

It was one of her wings that covered him. The swift-increasing light of dawn shimmered from it, with incredible hues of mauve and blue and purple.

Boyd's stiffened body trembled. Realization dazed him. It was this unbelievable bird-woman that the three gray planes had been attacking. No wonder he had thought it a very queer-looking machine!

Gratitude, perhaps, for his intervention, had impelled her to carry him from the dangerous proximity of his own burning plane.

But what manner of creature could she be?

Where, her dwelling?

His pains deadened with amazement, Boyd lifted his head farther yet. She was evidently still sleeping. Her slim, queerly woman-like body lay quiet on the yellow sand, close to his side. He glimpsed the folded silver pipe, whose music was soundless and deadly cold.

The other gleaming wing covered her, partially. But, beneath the fine silver down that lined it, he could see the soft slender curves of her body. The sleek golden down had almost the sheen of metal. He glimpsed the full up-tilted roundness of a golden breast.

Her sheer, strange loveliness caught his breath, pierced his side with a lance of pain.

His eyes came up to her face. Calm with her sleep, it was a soft golden oval. Pointed, exotic, incomparable in its beauty. Her mouth was small, but completely human, the lips moist and full and crimson—maddeningly kissable. Her nostrils were delicate and full; they widened regularly with her slow breathing.

The red helmet that followed the fine outline of her head and neck had the gleam of polished horn. Suddenly Boyd knew that it was no helmet. Its glistening scarlet scales were the living counterpart of human hair.

His eyes devouring her shining splendor, Boyd's blood raced faster. Almost he held his breath. He was afraid to try to move his numb stiff body again—

Afraid lest she fly away and leave him.

Eldritchly strange, she was yet more beautiful than any woman he had known. The burning wonder of her drove the old shadow of tragedy out of his heart. For the first time in nearly three years, he tasted the sharp bittersweet of life's desire.

Wholly non-human as this bright creature clearly was, he wanted to hold to her. He wanted to know all about her. About her home—far incredible place it must be! And he didn't want to lose her, ever.

Boyd tried to resist that tide of burning desire. He was, he tried to tell himself, still light-headed from the shock of his wound. Obviously, she was merely an avian mammal, or some order previously unknown. The trouble was simply that he had not gotten over that first incredible impression of the angel.

He ought to wake her. That would doubtless dispel his insane illusions. He would discover that she was merely an interesting sort of animal. A chance survivor, no doubt, of some evolutionary experiment that nature had abandoned in favor of more practical, if generally less artistic, types. She would be more intelligent, he was sure, than a horse or a dog. But she simply couldn't be the radiant, more-than-human being his imagination kept painting. That was impossible.

She stirred a little. And Boyd held his breath. A stark fear chilled him. He didn't want her to wake. He couldn't stand for her to wake. He was afraid of what she would turn out to be.

Nevertheless, she opened her eyes.

So doing, she captured Carter Boyd forever.

Her eyes were large, wide-set, and purple black. Their golden lids were somewhat different from the lids of human eyes, and they had an exotic slant. But their limpid boundless depths held all the intelligence, the gentle understanding, the lonely human soul—all that Boyd had yearned to see there, and despaired of.

SUFFERING and compassion were reflected in those depthless orbs. Boyd knew, from that first glance, that an agony of tragedy burdened her.

A sharp dread stabbed him. Now she would go. With a little anxious cry, Boyd reached with his good hand toward her sleek golden shoulder. But the great wings lifted, and swept her upright.

With an admirable gift of balance, she poised herself upon one delicate golden foot. The gay wings folded, into a purple cloak. The other small foot was lifted in front of her, on its slender tapered golden limb, like a hand. From the piquant golden face beneath the scarlet helmet, her great purple eyes looked sadly down at Boyd.

Fantastic creature! Half bird and half woman. Her elfin face reflected sorrow and also a kind of mocking whimsy. Bright and strange and beautiful, she had the heart-touching appeal of some Silly Symphony animal-creation of Disney's. The intelligence and the sadness in her eyes gave her a quality of humanity that made Boyd forget all her strangeness.

"Well?" She was so human that he couldn't help speaking to her. "Good morning, beautiful!"

She replied!

Her lips pouted into a red circle. She made soft melodious cooing sounds, that had the resonance of a golden bell. They seemed friendly and sympathetic.

But perhaps gestures would convey more meaning. Boyd contrived to sit upright. For a moment pain left him giddy. Then he pointed at his bandaged shoulder.

She hopped toward him, moving with an incredible ease and dexterity upon one hand-like foot. Deftly, with the other limb, she smoothed the bandage.

The golden bowls of her breasts were very close to him. His nostrils caught the clean, slight, haunting fragrance of her. He felt a sudden, savage desire to seize her in his arms. A lingering sense of her strangeness held him back, and the throbbing stiffness of his shoulder.

She hopped a little back from him. From her pouted lips pealed a melody of golden notes, in which Boyd groped vainly for some meaning. Then she spread her wings. The first cold arrow of sunlight, striking over the canyon rim, splintered on them into a mist of rainbow color.

She leapt easily upward, and soared over the cliff.

Left alone on the ledge, Boyd felt a sharp ache of loss keener than all his bodily pain. He wondered if she had gone forever back into the blank mystery from which she came. Or would she return?

Hunger and thirst were stirring in him. His eyes explored the ledge. It was a sand-covered shelf of rock, six feet wide. No man could climb the sheer dark cliff above. He crawled to the edge—and recoiled.

It was three hundred feet to the tumbled welter of black fallen boulders beneath.

"Whatever she is," he muttered, "she feels at home in high rocks! If she doesn't come back—"

Well, what was the difference. For a stranger to be dropped in this cruel desert was itself virtually a sentence of death. It didn't matter much how it came.

Carter Boyd wasn't used to giving up a struggle, even when hope seemed gone. But now there was no way to begin and nowhere to go. He wanted to see that winged being again—more, it seemed to him, than he had ever wanted anything before. But all he could do was to wait there on the ledge—

Until the madness of thirst would drive him to leap.

Climbing, the white sun magically banished the chill of night. The dark rocks began to pour a sweltering reverberation of heat down upon the ledge. The midday, here, would be sheer torture.

A few hardy flies buzzed for a time about his bandages. Then the mounting heat drove them to seek shade. Thirst made a dry fuzz in his throat. The slow drag of the hours became maddening.

Carter Boyd ceased to wonder if the winged being would return.

He began to wonder, instead, if she had ever existed.

CHAPTER IV

AIR ARMADA

FOR half a minute Jimmy Hall sat silent in the cockpit. Steady on the wheel, his big hands held the great bomber in level flight through the darkness. The red and green lights of the other plane floated amid the stars, above and ahead.

"Just follow, Jimmy," repeated the soft husky melody of Linda Gaylord's voice. "And you won't get hurt."

Above the low partition, that divided the cockpit from the navigation cabin, the muzzle of the gun held by the man she called Krošeć jabbed uncomfortably into the back of Hall's neck.

"*Ach, ja!*" affirmed Krošeć, who, despite the Balkan ring of his name, colored his meagre English with snarling German expletives. "Follow Yankee— or *Gott strafe* you!"

"Please, Jimmy!"

Hall had made no move, but some intuition filled the girl's voice with a sudden read anxiety.

"I don't want you to get hurt, Jimmy," she said urgently. "And you must see you haven't got a chance. I have a gun. Krošeć has one. And Mr. Jones's plane, ahead, is fully manned and armed—I can call him on the radio."

For answer, Jimmy Hall spun the wheel. He yanked hard back on it and kicked a rudder. The big bomber responded to her controls with that amazing readiness he had already learned to expect.

Red-haired Linda Gaylord was flung against his hard body, so violently that her breath went out with a gasp. Hall's big hand swooped away from the wheel, snatched at the dull gleam of her weapon. Her surprised fingers tightened on the little automatic, stubbornly. But he tore it easily away from her.

"*Ach, mein Go—*"

Krošeć's gutturals turned into a gasp of apprehension. For abruptly the little armored cabin was upside down and slanted sharply back. Krošeć fell on his head and tumbled back against the base of the gun turret.

The big bomber completed the roll. Krošeć was pitched back to the floor. Hall tipped the ship into a dive, and he slid forward again. But his dropped automatic came rattling ahead of him.

Hall twisted in his seat. Both men groped for the weapon. Hall's fingers scooped it up, brought it down with free and sufficient force upon the huge swarthy head of Krošeć.

"Well," he gasped, "that's—"

Turning back in his seat, to pull the

bomber out of the dive, he found that Linda Gaylord had caught up the telephone.

"Alec!" she was gasping into the mouthpiece. "This brute Hall has gone wild! Come back and show him——"

Dropping Krošeć's gun under his feet, with hers, Hall reached for the telephone. But Linda snatched his wrist with her free hand. Failing to push it back, she did something that surprised him. She sank her teeth into the heel of his thumb.

A grim smile, at that, lit Hall's lean face. A savage joy burned abruptly in his blue eyes. A little pain only heightened the fierce zest of combat. And it was no distaste for fighting that had led him to agree to join the military forces of China.

He released the big wheel with his left hand. Reaching across, he seized a very generous handful of Linda's red curls, and deliberately twisted.

Her teeth tightened savagely. Her slim white hands dropped the telephone, and made a clawing sweep at his face. To protect it, Hall dug his head hard into her body. He tightened his pulling grip on her hair, and her hands snatched into his own yellow shock, and her teeth set deeper into his hand. Her perfume made a heady fragrance in his nostrils. Twisting his head a little, against the thin silk sweater, he bared his teeth like a savage beast, and bit.

She gave a startled yelp, and her teeth let go.

For a moment she stared into his grinning face. She was breathless and trembling with fury. Then a sudden alarm froze her white features.

"Look out!" she snapped. "We'll crash!"

W I T H throttles wide, the big bomber was roaring down in a power dive toward the dark earth. In the pale starlight, nothing was visible beneath. But Hall knew that the mountains were waiting there, groping toward the sky with dark fingers of death.

Nevertheless, he let the gray plane plunge on down.

Linda's slim, desperate fingers seized his iron shoulder. In the glow of the instruments, her lovely face was pale with anxiety.

"Pull out of it!" she screamed above the booming of the motors. "Do you want to kill us both?"

Hall pulled up the plane, until a mirror showed him the lights of the other, dropping after him. He snapped off the flying lights of his own, let the big bomber roar on down.

At last the dim mighty flanks of the mountain range became darkly visible in the starlight. He cut the motors, so that the blue-and-yellow flare of the exhausts would not betray them. Pulling out of the dive, he wheeled through half a circle, dropped into the black shadows of a gorge.

Frozen at his side, the girl made a little gasping sound.

"Well, Jimmy," she breathed, "you can fly!"

Presently, when they had come out over the edge of a vast, night-blanketed valley, with the lights of towns and farms scattered far across it, Hall cut in the motors again. But he didn't snap on the flying lights.

The girl made no move when he reached across in front of her, and secured the dropped telephone. Her gray eyes were staring at him, with what seemed a startled admiration. Hall swung the plane northward, off the course upon which they had started.

"All right, darling." His low voice just carried above the motors. "Talk!"

"I'm sorry!" Her husky voice was small, frightened. "I'm sorry I bit you —I don't know what possessed me."

"That's all right, sweetheart!" Hall assured her. "Forget that part. But we've got another score to settle. You've been telling me a damned lot of lies. Now I want the truth."

Her gray eyes looked at him steadily. He had to give her credit for being cool enough.

"What do you want to know?"

"I signed up to fight for China. Now it is getting pretty obvious that I am not expected to do anything of the kind."

"That's true." Her smile was brilliant, hopeful, but a little uncertain. "We weren't very honest with you, Jimmy. Mr. Jones' organization has no connection whatever with the Chinese government."

"Then who is Mr. Jones?" Hall's voice was hard. "And what is he going to do with a lot of bombing planes?"

Her red head, that his fingers had tangled, shook very solemnly.

"I'm not to tell you that, Jimmy," she said positively. "Nothing can make me do it."

Hall ran lean fingers back through his own yellow hair. His blue eyes glanced swiftly behind him, to see that Krošeć was still unconscious, groaning. With a grim look on his face, he turned back to the girl.

"Get this, darling!" his voice rapped hard. "I was willing to fight for the Chinese, because I think right and justice is on their side. But if you think I'm going to join up with any mysterious gang of aerial racketeers—just think again!"

In the pale light, Linda Gaylord's lovely oval face smiled regretfully.

"That's the way I thought you'd feel, Jimmy," she said soberly. "That's why I tried to mislead you—we needed you so much. But it didn't work. I'm ashamed of it. Now I suppose there's just one thing to do."

HER shoulders made a tired little shrug. She pointed down toward a long straight row of headlights, like wide-strung beads, that marked a highway across the valley.

"The plane has landing lights," her weary voice said. "You can set her down, somewhere on the road. And get out. Some motorist will pick you up." She fumbled for her purse. "I've got money enough to get you back to your precious job."

Hall's lean jaw set.

"It isn't that easy. When you throw over a job like mine, it's gone. Anyhow, I don't like to quit anything in the middle."

She looked up again, hopefully.

"You won't have to quit. You can keep your job with the Trust, and draw your thousand a month. Krošeć will try to make trouble, but I guess we can handle him. Mr. Jones has much better prospects, just now, than Chiang Kai-shek."

"There are a good many things I would fight for," Hall told her. "But a thousand a month is not one of them."

"You won't be required to do any actual fighting," her clear voice promised. "You were hired as a training instructor. And you still have the privilege of quitting, on a week's notice." She leaned toward him. "You'll go on, Jimmy?"

"I'll go one," he said. "For one reason."

She smiled in the dim light, waiting.

"That reason, Linda, is you."

Her face was suddenly marble-cold.

"Just because you've pulled my hair, Mr. Hall"—her voice was brisk and icy—"don't let yourself expect too much. Please remember, so long as you are employed by the Trust, that you are my subordinate. Now, if you prefer to keep your job, I'll call Mr. Jones."

But Hall held the telephone out of her reach.

"What I ought to do," he said grimly, "is to set this ship down somewhere in the woods, and give you some lessons in manners. But that would break several laws. I'm going to go ahead, into this mess. Because I want to know what kind of dirty work your Mr. Jones has got on foot. And because I've got a hunch, sweetheart, that before the end you're going to need some help!"

He gave her the phone.

"Alec," he heard her report, "the brute has come to terms. We are turning west. Will contact you at dawn. . . . No, Alec, dear, I'm quite all right. . . . No, darling, I'm sure that Mr. Hall will be a very useful man."

Hall saw that the bull-like Krošeć was reviving, beginning to moan and fumble about the dark cabin. He interrupted the girl.

"Your rat is coming to," he told her. "You had better inform him that hostilities have ceased—if you don't want him exterminated!"

The sun overtook them far out over the gray, white-glinting Pacific. The girl had talked at intervals to the other plane. Presently it appeared, a tiny fleck above the flat empty southern horizon, and bore steadily northward to resume its place ahead of them.

For intervals of two hours to his four, Linda Gaylord had taken the controls. She proved an alert and skilful pilot. Fatigue was beginning to hollow her gray eyes a little. But, in the daylight, Hall was fascinated anew by her vital, red-haired loveliness.

How such a girl could have become involved in this unholy-seeming affair, he still couldn't imagine. But he still believed that she would need his aid, eventually.

The man Krošeć hunched broodingly behind them. He was an enormous man, very dark, pockmarked, hairy as an ape, with black, malevolent eyes. Hall guessed that he had picked up his Teutonic expletives from some choleric Prussian officer. His temple was blood-matted and swollen, and his sullen eyes dwelt upon Hall in baleful resentment of the blow.

"Tell your hyena to quit grinning at me like he wanted to eat me alive," he advised the girl once, "or I'll drop him out for a bath—"

Krošeć, who had overheard as Hall intended, let out a savage roar:

"*Gott und Himmel!* Vait—chust vait till we get to base—you *verdammt* American peeg!"

And Linda shook her head at Hall, gravely.

"You had better not quarrel with Captain Krošeć," she warned. "He is one of Mr. Jones's most trusted officers."

ALTHOUGH they didn't quite follow the course that he had plotted, Hall soon guessed that their destination, in fact, lay somewhere in Asia. In thirty-four hours, he knew they must have covered something over seven thousand miles. The days lagged, since they flew with the sun, and darkness of the second night was just falling, when Linda told him they would land in half an hour.

"We're somewhere," he said, "over the Gobi."

Fatigue had drawn her white face a little. The red curls were tangled. But the bright, inviting beauty of her had grown into him, so that it was now a kind of ache in his heart.

"Jimmy," she warned again, "you'll live a lot longer, and be happier in your work for the Trust, if you don't try to find out too much." Her clear tone broke. "And — I hope you live, Jimmy!"

The wing-lights of the other plane waggled a signal. Flood-lights picked out a landing field, below. Circling, following the other plane in, Hall stared in silent amazement.

What might lie beyond the lights, he

could not tell. But along the edge of the field, he saw an endless row of huge gray bombers, like this he flew. Sixty, he estimated.

A secret aerial Armada!

Here, waiting unsuspected in the desert, was a flying threat to the peace of the world. What power had created it? For what sinister purpose?

Hall shuddered, and his blue eyes leapt anxiously to Linda Gaylord. This thing looked far worse than he had ever guessed. How far was she involved? What did all this mean to her?

His anxious voice boomed out, "Linda—"

Her white fingers closed his lips.

"Remember, Jimmy! If you value your life—don't ask questions!"

Gigantic Krošeć loomed like a black shadow behind him.

"*Nein!*" he snarled. "But when we are on der ground, you'll find out something. *Ja,* Yankee deffil!"

CHAPTER V

DESERT EDEN

CARTER BOYD thought for a moment that he was delirious, when a silken rustle made him open his eyes against the blinding glare, and he saw that the bright-winged creature had dropped beside him on the sand-banked ledge.

For she had brought him water.

Her many-colored wings had made the rustle, as they folded back into the odd imperial sedateness of a purple cloak. She stood, with that incredible effortless poise, on one delicate foot.

In the other hand-like foot, lifted before her unselfconsciously exposed breasts, she held a porcelain water pot. Moving with an infinitely light and easy grace, she hopped toward Boyd. His sound arm reached trembling to take the little covered jar.

He rinsed his dry bitter mouth, gulped a few precious swallows, and then offered it to her. She refused it. Her red lips voiced reassuring and solicitous bell-notes. She gestured for him to drink again.

"Thanks, beautiful!" Gratefully, Boyd drained the little pot. "This is something like Elijah and the ravens. Only, darling, the ravens couldn't have had quite your figure!"

Refreshed somewhat, he stared at the little jar. It was an exquisite thing, the finely crackled glaze blending soft shades of green, purple, and gray. A Chün piece, he thought, of the Kuan type. From the Sung Dynasty. Centuries old. Priceless.

His brain still fogged with pain and heat, Boyd looked up at the tapered golden face, watching him with elfin interest.

"Where'd you get this?" he demanded.

The mellow chime of her voice replied incomprehensibly. Her gleaming golden limb pointed off into space, and then made a series of puzzling gestures.

"Sorry, sweetheart!" gasped Boyd. "But I don't savvy the lingo—and it's too hot to argue, anyhow." He sank back upon the burning sand. "Not that it makes much difference if you've got a whole museum of old pots, somewhere. This country may be all right for golden angels. But it's no place for a winged white man."

For answer, she skipped lightly toward him. Her soft golden fingers seized his good arm, lifted it gently over the red bright carapace that covered her head. She made him rise.

Boyd tried to forget his sick despair. He relaxed against her. Still he had a haunting suspicion that all this wasn't real—that probably he had happened to glimpse a buzzard, soaring as it waited for the feast; that delirium had created everything else.

But even that doubt didn't trouble him, now. The delicate perfume of her was intoxicating in his nostrils. A kind of giddiness dulled his pains.

Convulsively, ignoring the stabbing protest from his side, he pressed her sleek body closer. He couldn't breathe. His heart was pounding. He felt her smooth golden limbs fold around him in a close embrace. A happy cooing sound throbbed softly from her small crimson mouth.

Boyd swayed, in a pleasant gray haze. His head was spinning. This was more and more dream-like, but that didn't matter. Thirstily he turned his face, seeking her lips.

Then Carter Boyd got the surprise of his life.

For her splendid wings spread abruptly. One mighty beat toppled them both off the ledge. Boyd took one look at the pile of gigantic black boulders, hundreds of feet below, and shut his eyes.

He was used to flying—but not to being carried by a winged woman.

He was not a heavy man, but he thought his weight must be greater than her own. It was clear now that she must have carried him to the ledge, in the first place. But, obviously, he was a very heavy burden for her. The bright wings beat heavily. Her breath soon became a swift, whistling sound.

Boyd opened his eyes again. They were still dropping toward the talus slope. As they gained speed, however, they ceased to fall. And presently, turning up the canyon, they rose again laboriously.

Boyd's mind still had a feverish incoherence. As soon as he discovered they weren't going to be immediately shattered on the rocks, he decided that this was a very pleasant experience.

HE liked the rhythmic beat of strong shoulder muscles, under the fine glossy velvet of her golden down. There was mad intoxication in the warm pliant pressure of her breasts. Her faint haunting perfume set his senses to spinning again.

He managed to brush her red lips, with his. He looked into her exotic slanted eyes, so close above his own. Huge and dark, they seemed to smile at him, tenderly. It was a strange feel-that seized him—a passion as strange as its object—but Boyd knew that he loved this incredible being, hopelessly.

His soul was plunged into as abyss of emotion far deeper and stronger and more intense than the madness of desire burning in him. He felt a sharp pity for her evident exhausted weariness, the pain of her effort. And he hungered desperately for communication with her.

He wanted terribly to know all about her, to share all the burden of her unspoken tragedy. Fiercely he desired to bring back to her the happiness he knew she had lost.

Presently she alighted to rest upon a stark naked pinnacle of red, wind-worn sandstone. There was just footing for one. Boyd stood upon his own feet, and supported her in the curve of his sound arm.

Her bright wings drooped wearily, merely beating feebly, now and then, to fan the hot air about them. Her body, velvet-soft against him, moved to her swift breath.

A sudden impulsive joy of possession made Boyd squeeze her golden body against his own, so hard that her racing heart seemed to thump against his own flesh. His own fired pulse leapt faster.

Avidly, he again sought her lips.

But the flamboyant wings made a protesting little flutter, and she tried to draw away from him. Boyd held her, feeling that she was more to him than life.

"My beautiful—" he was sobbing, "my incredible—angel!"

Her strange purple eyes looked up at his face, seeming puzzled at first. She made a throbbing, questioning note, and then a trill of melody that sounded infinitely sad. A tear flashed down, suddenly, across her golden cheek. And she clung shuddering to Boyd. Her lips pressed hard against his own, until they both were breathless.

Abruptly her wings spread again, and carried them off the pinnacle.

He was insane, Boyd told himself. Probably going into delirium, from the fever of his pulsating wound. And still he hadn't got over that first startled idea of the angel. Obviously, however, this flaming being was very far from either human or conventional angel. It seemed most unwise to let his feelings get wrapped up in her.

"But what the hell?" he muttered.

A man might as well walk into a blazing forest, and say that he had better not get burned. He couldn't help what her eerie beauty did to him. He drew his arm tighter over the rippling velvet of her smooth shoulders. He tried to forget everything except the warm intoxication of her breasts against his body, and her maddening perfume.

He woke out of a pain-drugged dream of bliss, when she alighted again. She slipped away from his arm, and stood on one foot beside him, her wings hanging wearily. Boyd let her go with sharp regret.

His first glimpse of what lay beneath, however, had restored the hope that had died with the falling of his plane. Then he had abandoned life. Here, in the valley below him, was the promise of life restored.

They had alighted on the ragged lip of a canyon's scarp. Black time-shattered crags plunged down vertically. Half a thousand feet beneath them,

bright as some jewel in this dark desert hell, lay a fragment of paradise.

Here was water, in the waterless waste!

It burst from a higher gorge, at the upper end of the dark-walled canyon. A thin thread of silver, it fell. White spray glinted where it struck a green and ancient channel. Below, it ran to fill a broad crystal pool.

Man had been here, and gone.

The channel was straight, and walled with masonry. A man-made dam held the pool. Men must have set the rows of gnarled and ancient fruit trees. The little fields, yellow and green with wild grains, must have been terraced by men.

GRAY walls of crumbling stone rose on the farther slope. Boyd recognized the compounds and the shattered temple hall and the ruined pagodas of a Buddhist monastery.

In the far-gone years, Boyd knew, some little wandering band of monks must have come upon the hidden treasure of the fall. Secure from the world, they had built their cloistered, self-sufficient community.

What had happened to them?

Clearly, they had been gone for many years. Perhaps some landslide had obliterated the trail, so that the celibate community dwindled and perished, forgotten. Perhaps the monks had been wiped out by Mongol raiders—but such vandals would hardly have left the Sung water jar.

That didn't matter. For here was precious water in the pool. Shelter in the abandoned buildings. Food, even —for the gnarled old trees bore fruit; there were garden plants and grains gone wild; once-domesticated fowls were scratching beneath a pomegranate tree.

Boyd turned grinning to his companion.

"So here we are, beautiful!" he whispered. "A little Eden, just for you and me!"

An answering smile illuminated her elfin face. Through golden lids, her great slanted dark eyes looked happily at Boyd. She made a melodious coo of reply, that made Boyd say:

"The first thing, darling, will be some lessons in your language!"

Abruptly, then, she made a little choked and anxious sound. The bright wings folded close she flung her golden body shuddering into a little hollow in the rock. Tiny yellow fingers motioned frantically at Boyd.

As he dropped, he understood.

Far-off, he heard the humming of an airplane. A deep and distant sound, it rose and fell, rose and fell, in waves of menace. At last, following the fear-distended eyes of his companion, Boyd glimpsed the plane.

It was drifting above a dark jagged ridge of treeless mountains in the south. The same type, he believed, as the gray ships he had fought. That battle, he knew, had not ended the danger that his winged companion feared so terribly.

The strange plane dropped at last beyond the far dry mountains, but its passing had clouded the bright promise of this desert Eden with a black and mysterious shadow of peril.

CHAPTER VI

HELL IN CANS

KROSEC was first to climb out of the big bomber, when Jimmy Hall had landed it on that flood-lit field somewhere in the Gobi, had taxied it into place at the end of that long ominous gray line of similar planes.

Linda Gaylord's foot slipped, as the big American pilot helped her down from the door in the armored gray fuselage. Her yielding body was crushed for a moment against his shoulder, her red fragrant hair was in his face. His arms squeezed her.

"Don't—Jimmy!"

Apprehension was in her gasp.

"If Alec saw us—you wouldn't live a day!"

Hall set her on her feet, grinning. With a quick, anxious look after Krošeć, she stepped a little away from him.

"First thing," she whispered, "we must report to Alec—the man you know as Mr. Jones. He is Count Alexandrov Renvic. He prefers to be called simply *The Alexander.* He will expect a military salute."

She walked swiftly in front of Hall toward a little group standing about the other plane. A hard-bitten, desperate lot of men, they looked to Hall. Half of them, probably, had the stamp of Renvic's and Krošeć's own Balkan race. The rest came from everywhere. They were all in gray uniforms. Most of the Balkan officers were young. They carried themselves with an arrogant, dashing swagger.

Just now, however, everybody was being respectful to the lean pale supercilious man who had been presented to Hall as Mr. Smithson Jones. He wore black, and the lights gleamed on his bare black head. He seemed to strut, before the attentive officers. His green eyes lifted sharply at the approach of Hall and the girl.

"Linda!" His metallic voice rang possessively. "Were you injured by zis man?"

Linda Gaylord showed none of the awed respect of the men in gray. She walked quickly up to Renvic, and put her slim arms around him in a familiar embrace. Boiling inwardly, Hall still noticed that she offered only her cheek to be kissed.

"No, Alec darling," she was saying. "Mr. Hall was naturally angry, when he learned that we had deceived him. Captain Krošeć pulled his gun, before I had time to explain, and Mr. Hall took it away from him. But everything is all right, now—But where's Dad?"

The narrowed green eyes looked very sharply from Linda to Hall.

"I am told Doctair Gaylord ees not back from his evening walk." The sleek black head jerked impatiently into the darkness, westward. "Down in the gorge, they say he has found the remains of some greater monster. Fool, digging up old bones in the dark! But he weel be here."

Renvic turned abruptly from the girl. Snapping out Hall's name, he omited most of the *h,* so that it was nearly:

" 'All!"

"Yes, sir," said Hall.

Renvic waited for something. His breath drew in sharply. His pale arrogant face began to turn a little pink. Linda Gaylord looked urgently at Hall, Whispering under her breath:

"Salute!"

Hall brought his arm up, in a brisk military salute. But the green-eyed man failed to return it. His arrogant appearance touched off a kind of fuse in Hall, who said loudly:

"Yes, Mr. Jones?"

Renvic stiffened. His narrow, rather feeble chin drew down. His thin face turned a darker red. His breath caught angrily, and Hall expected something violent. But the sharp metallic voice said merely:

"I am zee Alexander. Forget Mr. Jones. And remember to salute me."

"Yes, sir," Hall said flatly.

"Your rank here will be lieutenant. Your duties will be to train my aviation personnel. Tomorrow you will report for orders, to Captain Krošeć. Now you may go to your quarters."

And Renvic wheeled toward the glowering Krošeć.

Hall's head jerked toward the hairy man, and he whispered to Linda:

"Won't that be a picnic?"

Her gray eyes mocked him. "You asked for it!"

THEN she turned suddenly away from him, toward a short bald fat man who came waddling and puffing into the light. The little man wore a monocle in a red moon face that was set with chronic irritation. A white topi hung from his neck. White duck shorts revealed that his fat sun-reddened legs were remarkably bowed.

"Dad!" Hall failed to see any family likeness, but the girl flung herself into his arms. "Dad, I'm so glad to be back! You are all right? You held my post?"

"No trouble, dear."

Adjusting his monocle, which her enthusiastic kiss had got out of place, the little man turned to Renvic.

"Alexander," he said in a rather shrill voice, "I am glad to see you back. Now I can take full time to excavate my discovery. I have found a complete skeleton of my new species, *Cycloptosaurus Gaylordi.* I am anxious to complete its recovery, before we must return to the rock. It is a find that will make my place—"

Renvic broke in with an abrupt question:

"Has the fugitive been found?"

Gaylord looked a little ruffled.

"No," he said. "But my *Cycloptosaurus—*"

"We've got to find her," rapped Renvic. "I'll send out more planes, tomorrow. And offer bigger rewards to the Mongol spies."

Gaylord's bare, sun-burned head was nodding.

"Indeed," he shrilled, "a living witness would be an invaluable addition to the inscriptions and the relics. But give your men orders to handle her with caution. Her reactions are largely incomprehensible to me, but previously I suspected a suicidal tendency."

"You may go back to your work, Doctair," rapped Renvic. "I want those formulas on the G-ray.— If we catch her, Krošeć will know how to make her talk, and I need that freezing weapon."

Standing unnoticed at the edge of the group, Hall had been listening with a good deal of interest. Talk of the Rock and this fugitive was all enigma. But if Krošeć were going to handle her, then her situation was not to be envied.

Now Renvic discovered him, and the green eyes blazed.

" 'All," his metallic voice twanged ominously, "I dismissed you to your quartairs!"

"So you did, sir," Hall agreed. "But you neglected to inform me where my quarters are."

Renvic glared for a moment, spun on his heel.

"Captain Krošeć, find an orderly and have Lieutenant Hall conducted to his tent."

Hall found the next morning interesting. A gray uniform was provided him. He ate in a long mess-tent, with his new, oddly-assorted fellow officers. He stood in line with them, under Krošeć's belligerent inspection.

Meantime, however, he saw more of his new surroundings. This secret aviation base occupied a long flat gravel plateau. Eastward, it sloped toward a waste of yellow crescent dunes. The western rim fell more abruptly, into a tumbled waste of bad lands—a welter of canyons and gorges, of bare cliffs and pyramids and pinnacles—a lifeless hostile wilderness that erosion had carved from red and yellow clays and sandstones and shales.

Several hundred officers and men were quartered in the city of gray tents beside the field—obviously, however, Renvic had far too few trained crews to man all the sixty planes. These were several large buildings of white sheet-metal and native sandstone. Arsenals, probably; hangars; supply depots.

A big castle-like building, of gray sandstone, stood apart on the plateau's upper end. Precious water sprayed a scrap of green lawn about it. Above it flew a curious flag—on a gray field, there was a symbol that looked like a black-winged boulder, with a golden crown above it.

That, Hall guessed, must be Renvic's dwelling.

Another thing puzzled him. On the rim of the plateau, between castle and camp, stood a spidery tower of white metal. Swung atop it, a hundred feet high, was something that looked like an elongated silver egg.

A black spot like an eye was visible in the smaller end of that streamlined case. The thing had somehow an ominous look, as if it might be a weapon. Hall failed to guess its nature. He realized that it would be very difficult to heed Linda's warning about asking questions.

THIS whole establishment presented a baffling riddle. Who was Renvic? What was he going to do with a private flying army? Where had he got the money to equip it? For Hall knew that this sinister armada must represent an investment of at least fifteen or twenty million dollars.

It happened that he got one significant clue.

After the inspection, Krošeć ordered Hall to be ready to fly, at ten o'clock, and then went roaring away to Renvic's castle on a gray motorcycle. Hall was waiting, at the edge of the field, when one of the big, graceful gray planes came in.

A gray-painted armored truck came lumbering down from the castle, and roared out to the side of the plane. Guards with sub-machine guns clambered out, and stood about alertly while some load was being transferred from plane to truck.

Curious, Hall walked out to see what they were unloading. It was none of his business. He realized that the act was probably dangerous. But nobody stopped him.

He saw several heavy, bulky burlap bundles. Then the men in gray staggered under a bright-colored, brass-bound box that looked like an antique coffer. When that was in the truck, they began passing out short round rods of gleaming yellow metal. The rods looked small. From the apparent effort it took to move them, Hall knew that they were gold.

Gold! And a coffer of treasure!

Loot of some conquered empire— but what empire had Renvic conquered? Had he joined the Japanese invaders in the rapine of China? Hall doubted it— the bright decorations on the coffer were definitely not Chinese.

Nor had he ever seen gold molded into rods, anywhere.

Still watching, it chanced that he saw the deft fingers of a swarthy little man —some sort of Eurasian, apparently, for his panting curses were in French— slip something bright into a gray uniform. When the unloading was done, Hall approached and demanded his name.

Turning white, the little man stammered:

"Du—Duval. But have mercy on me, lieutenant!"

"Report to my tent," Hall ordered him, "in five minutes."

He returned to his tent. Five minutes later, the little Eurasian lifted the flap. In a trembling hand he held out a small bright object.

"*Mon Dieu!*" he gasped. "Take it, *monsieur*. Take it, and say nothing to the Alexander." His voice was husky with dread. "He would give me to that *cochon* Krošeć, to be destroyed!"

Hall reached out his hand.

"Say nothing, Duval," he said. "And I'll see that this reaches the proper hands."

"*Eh bien!*" The fellow dropped the trinket into his fingers. "Thank you, *monsieur!*"

Strange jewel, indeed!

Alone in the tent, Hall examined it. The long chain, of sparkling crimson links, looked as if it must have been cut, by some marvel of the jeweler's art, from one monster pigeon's-blood ruby.

Swung from the chain was a heavy little figure of enameled metal. A most curious figure. For it represented an incredible thing—a creature half bird and half woman!

The golden body, with its delicate limbs and full-rounded, up-tipped breasts, was almost human. But the legs ended with tiny hands, instead of feet. And the upper limbs were two spread wings, lined with white platinum, enameled on the outside with gorgeous colors. The woman-like, delicate head was covered with a close-fitting red cap, and the eyes, oddly slanted, were twin purple sapphires.

That little figurine was the most puzzling object that Hall had ever looked upon. For the minute, painstaking detail of it convinced him instantly that it was no mere fantasy of an imaginative artist, done in precious metal. He knew that it was an accurate copy of a living original.

But what an original!

None, certainly, known to biology. If some species of bird had followed a unique evolutionary trend, for millions of years, until they became bird-mammals, the result might have been such creatures as this. But where on earth could that have happened?

A precious thing, the jewel. No wonder it had tempted Duval! Hall decided that he had better see that it got back to Renvic at the first opportunity. His interest had been in what it could tell him, but it raised more questions than it asked. Doubtless it would be fatal to have it found on him. If little Duval should talk—

BACK on the field, he found two bombers being warmed up. Krošeć returned with Renvic, in a long gray armored limousine. A truck, following, carried the bright cylinders of two small bombs. One of the bombs was loaded into the recessed racks of each plane— racks equipped to hold at least eighty similar bombs.

" 'All!" Renvic waited for him to salute. "Before you take up your duties, lieutenant, of training my men," the metallic voice rapped, "it ees wise that you should become familiar with our equipment."

"Yes, sir."

"Therefore, you will accompany Captain Krošeć on a test flight thees morning. You will each drop one of our new G-bombs. The forces radiated when these bombs explode increase temporarily the effect of gravity on objects within range. For safety, you weel drop them from an altitude of at least fifteen thousand feet, and then dive to observe the effect on your objective. You weel receive further orders from Captain Krošeć aloft, by radio."

Krošeć's plane roared away ahead. Hall was at the wheel of his own, which was manned by the swarthy Balkan officers. One of them operated the radio.

Hall had supposed that the "objective" would be merely a patch of desert. But Krošeć led the way southward. After two hours, they came to a narrow river, followed down it at high altitude until they were over the brown dots and gray ribbons and green patchwork that marked a little mud village.

Above that, Krošeć dropped his G-bomb.

Tense with a horrified indignation, Hall followed the other bomber down, to see what had happened. They found the village obliterated. Mud huts were shattered as if a great invisible heel had trod upon them. In the flattened fields lay the crushed bodies of peasants and their oxen. Women and babies lay in the rutted streets, dark pools of blood squeezed out of them, as if they had been grapes in some hellish press.

The man at the radio relayed an order to Hall:

"Lieutenant, you will drop your G-bomb on the next village, down the stream. Captain Krošeć's command."

But Hall's vision was obscured with a red mist of anger. His big tanned body was trembling.

"Tell Krošeć," he shouted, "to guess again!"

And he wheeled the bomber back toward Renvic's secret base.

"Lieutenant," sharply warned the officer at the radio, "this will be mutiny. The Alexander will have you shot for this. Captain Krošeć requests me to tell you—"

"Cease communication," Hall ordered savagely. "I'll see Renvic and Krošeć when we land."

But even in his wrath, he could see that things looked very dark ahead.

CHAPTER VII

SHADRONA OF SHAR

AFTER the ominous whisper of the passing plane had ceased, Carter Boyd's companion lifted him on her brilliant wings again, and they glided down to begin the strange bitter-sweet of their existence in the dark-walled valley of the abandoned monastery.

Sweet, even through the fever and delirium that came from Boyd's infected shoulder, because every day brought its new revelations of the surpassing wonder, the humanity of soul, and the understanding devotion of his winged savior.

Even before they could talk, he was certain that she had come to return his own blazing passion with some feeling far deeper than mere gratitude.

Bitter, along with the sweet, because of the tragedy and the fears that haunted her. The abiding shadow of great sorrow never left her limpid purple eyes. If a living thing had been haunted, Boyd felt, it was she.

He could never solve the riddle of her dreads.

Always she watched the narrow rift of sky above the canyon walls. Often she silenced him, to listen, while a strange tensity of apprehension froze her golden face. He knew she was consumed with dread of the gray planes that hunted her.

Boyd made her let him examine the cold-weapon, whose telescoped silver tube she wore slung from her shoulders. Its control must have involved those eerie half-guessed telepathic powers beyond his first vision of her, but the mechanism itself appeared rather simple.

A tiny rotor, in the mouthpiece, was turned by the breath. That drove what looked like a miniature dynamo, which was connected to a long spidery helix. Boyd could make nothing of its principles, and he stared in new amazement at his companion's demonstration of its weird power.

Her golden fingers flashed across the intricate keys, faster than he could follow them. Above the faint hum of the rotor, he sensed rather than heard the thin eldritch wailing of piercing melodic minors. And he shivered to sudden, bone-piercing cold.

Frost snapped and glittered in the air before the silver tube. A gnarled little tamarisk was quickly frozen, chilled to such a temperature that swift condensation covered it with bright silver.

Amazing weapon!

Only later, when Boyd saw it tested again in the darkness, did he attempt even a guesswork explanation. Then he saw intense weird gleams of fluorescence bursting from the freezing objects, and knew that they were emitting "hard" radiations.

Incredible discovery! It meant that in the path of that eerie soundless vibration the normal direction of entropy-change was reversed. Heat, before the weapon, was transmuted into X-rays, perhaps even into electrons and atoms! And objects drained of heat were cold.

An instrument of ghastly potentialities. But the frightened gestures of the winged woman made clear that she regarded its power as nothing, against all the weapons of her mysterious enemies.

On thing that deeply troubled Boyd was her attitude toward clouds. Let the smallest wisp of white vapor float into the ribbon of blue desert sky above the cliffs, and she would stare at it with an incomprehensible intensity of interest. Sometimes she soared on her wings, to get a better view. She would return to him, shuddering with dread, anxious for the shelter of his arms.

Often, after a cloud had passed, Boyd found her slumped in some lonely corner of the ancient courts and gardens, the red carapace of her head covered with her wings' bright arches, shaken with inconsolate sobs.

But for those shadows of fear and strange wonder, their life in the old monastery would have been completely idyllic.

For they found all the needs of life.

Over part of the abandoned buildings, the roofs were still intact. In the dust choked ruins, besides a great many stone Buddhas, prayer wheels, and moldering manuscripts, they found such useful articles as cooking vessels and garden tools.

At first there were a few hungry days. But as soon as Boyd was able to move about, they found an abundance of fruits, grain, vegetables, and wild poultry.

Boyd's keenest desire was for some weapon with which he might help to defend his winged companion, if her mysterious enemies should ever discover them. But his automatic had been lost. The ancient monks must have been men of peace, for all his searching of the ruins yielded not even a spear. He was forced to content himself with a fire-pointed wooden lance.

Boyd had hoped to learn her language. His first serious attempt, however, to imitate her pealing golden word-sounds failed disastrously.

It was after he was almost completely recovered. He was sitting on the low, crumbling stone wall about one of the ancient gardens, which he had just dug up with an old bronze hoe.

HIS companion's golden body was poised, as usual, on one small foot before him. His attempt to imitate her voice seemed to agitate her queerly. She trembled. Her breath made a piping whistle. Suddenly Boyd realized that she was laughing at him.

But she understood his effort. Boyd, to his surprise, discovered that she had already picked up, apparently from the casual comments that he had never expected her to understand, a number of English words.

For she pointed a tiny golden finger at him, while from the red circle of her pursed lips came a pealing:

"Ae! Ae!"

After a puzzled instant, Boyd touched himself excitedly.

"I," he repeated. "I!"

"Ae!" She spun about the garden in a little skipping dance. Then she pressed the little hand against her gleaming golden breasts. Her bell-tones throbbed something that sounded like "Boo'fool!"

"Beautiful!" Boyd exclaimed. That was what he had so often called her. She skipped delightedly toward him. He caught her in his arms, kissed her. "My wonderful darling, you truly are!"

"Dar'in'!" she throbbed, and touched the soft sleek velvet of her body again. "Boo'fool! Dar'in'! Shadrona!"

"Shadrona!" Boyd repeated softly. "That's your name!" She danced about him in delight, as light and swift as some wraight of colored light. "Mine's Carter Boyd."

Her tiny finger touched him, and she cooed:

"Ae i' Car'er Boy'!"

Each aquiver with eagerness to know about the other, they carried on the lessons. Shadrona had some difficulty with English consonants, but soon she could render them with a surprising accuracy. She learned swiftly and forgot nothing.

It was easy for Boyd to teach her the names of most objects within reach or sight, a good many verbs of action, a few simple adjectives. But it proved appallingly difficult to communicate the question whose answer he wanted so desperately:

"Where did you come from?"

When at last she understood, the great eyes of Shadrona darkened again with sorrow. Hopping to Boyd's side, she clutched his fingers with a tight, trembling little golden hand. She clung to him, shaken with a wind of nameless terror.

"Where, Shadrona?" he repeated.

Detaching her hand for a moment, she pointed at a thin feather of cloud drifting high above the black cliffs.

"Shar!" sobbed her golden voice. "You—from Shar!"

Still she had not grasped the complexities of pronouns. *Ae* was a name for Boyd, *You* a name for herself.

"You, Shadrona of Shar." Her slanted eyes were bright with tears. Her head bowed. Meaninglessly, her low voice moaned, "Shar no Shar. Shar no Shar."

Holding her fast in his arms, Boyd kissed her.

"You don't mean, darling, that you came from a cloud?" His head shook wearily. "What are you afraid of? If I only knew——"

He smoothed the sand at his feet, sketched the outline of airplane. So that there could be no mistake, he even added the insigne of winged rock and crown that he had seen on the gray attacker's fuselage. That meant something to her. Trembling, she sobbed tragically:

"Shar is Shar!"

Suddenly, then, she burst into a fit of wailing. Her cries were thin, prolonged, utterly heartbroken. Boyd was shaken. The tears of any woman were torture to him, Shadrona's sheer agony.

He picked her quivering golden body up in his arms. Her bright wings dragged, hopelessly. He rocked her, like a child. At last, to his infinite relief, she ceased her cries. Silently, she lifted her tear-streaked golden face, for him to kiss.

Thereafter, Boyd was careful to avoid any too-sensitive spot on her past. He only hoped that their refuge might remain undiscovered.

At first, he had made plans for an attempt to take Shadrona out to civilization. But he began to fear that the inevitable notoriety would make her more

unhappy than ever. She was clearly unwilling to leave their valley. And Boyd himself became more and more content with the life they led.

There was more wonder in her small golden body than he had found in all the world. More surprise in the continual revelations of her mind, her love, than in all the cities of men.

"Shadrona," he whispered one bright morning, when he sat on the crumbling garden wall, with her soft-lined wing across his shoulder, and the velvet warmth of her body in his arms, "if we live our lives out here, we'll still die the happiest beings on this planet!"

"So!" she cooed, that being her word of assent. "So——"

Then she stiffened and shuddered against him. Turning pale, her lips parted to a low, moaning sound. Her golden hand pointed. And Boyd saw the big gray plane, black muzzles of machine guns jutting evilly from its fighting turret. Silent, with all its motors cut, it was gliding down to the field below the pool.

Boyd knew that their sojourn in the desert Eden was ended.

CHAPTER VIII

SPIES MUST DIE!

THE two bombers dropped to the secret base, and taxied back into the line. Jimmy Hall's anger was turning more and more to apprehension, but his horror at the fate of the unwarned village remained.

That helpless Chinese village, shattered by the uncanny purplish blast of the G-bomb, seemed to suggest what might lie in store for all the world.

"There was no danger, sir," the young officer who had been his co-pilot ventured, uneasily. "We've tried the

G-bombs before. It is always blamed on the Japanese."

A curt word silenced him. Hall clambered out. He saw dark, bull-like Krošeć striding toward him, and waited.

"Vell, *v e r d a m m t Schweinhund!*" snarled the man. His hairy face showed a sudden gloating grin. "Mutiny! *Ja,* I think this will be the finish of you!"

Hall's blue eyes were frosty.

"We'll see."

Some word must have been radioed ahead. For in a moment the armored limousine drew up beside them. Renvic sprang out, followed by several officers in gray. His thin autocratic face was white, the green eyes blazing with anger.

"Lieutenant 'All!" he rapped metallicly, "I hear zat you refuse to obey my orders."

Hall stared back at him.

"If you'll read my contract," he said flatly, "you won't find anything that requires me to bomb defenseless villages."

Renvic's thin hands made a savage gesture, as if they tore up the document.

"Contract?" he rasped. "Bah!"

Hall caught his breath.

"If that's your attitude, Renvic—I quit. I won't murder helpless women and children. What's more, I won't train other men to murder them. Consider this notice of my resignation."

Renvic trembled.

"You've come too far to quit." The green eyes narrowed. "Lieutenant 'All, I am placing you under military arrest. I will give you twenty-four hours to reconsider."

"I don't need them," rapped Hall. "I'm no murderer today, and I'll not be one tomorrow."

He kept his voice steady and his tanned face grimly set. Inside, however, a cold sickness filled him. He had already learned far too much to be allowed to leave here—alive.

But Renvic seemed to make an effort to control his wrath.

"See here, lieutenant." His pale face assumed an icy smile. "I need such men as you. Follow me, and I can promise you such a career as you never dreamed of."

Hall watched him, grim-faced.

"You have seen a G-bomb," rapped Renvic. "You must realize that one plane, carrying eighty of them, could crush New York, say, to a pancake of bloody brick and metal. You must realize that these sixty planes could conquer the world—or destroy it."

"If—" whipped back the frosty voice of Hall, "you can get the men to fly them."

"I've got the men." Renvic trembled. "And I'll get them trained." He seemed to choke, made another effort to wipe the anger off his face. "However, lieutenant, the G-bombs represent less than half the power I have gathered to conquer the world for the new Alexander."

Jimmy Hall waited, trying hard to keep any show of eagerness from his stiff face.

Renvic's black arm swept back toward the silver tower.

"There is a G-ray projector. At a hundred miles, even, it can crush down a hostile plane with double its weight. At ten miles it can crush men into dough, and make the solid earth flow like water to close the trenches over them, and cause battleships to sink as if a giant hand thrust them down!"

The green eyes of Renvic were glaring at Hall, with a terrible fanatic light. His thin face was marble, with a mad elation.

"Now, lieutenant!" His voice was breathless, high. "What do you say? What do you say if I tell you that I have another stronghold—a secret fortress that no enemy can ever discover? What do you say if I tell you that the G-weapons are not all?"

HIS white face twisted into a demoniac mask.

"For there are other, greater secrets, lieutenant. One is a ray of freezing death, that could congeal a whole city. I withhold my power, until they also are mastered. Then truly the new Alexander will conquer!"

He swung closer to Hall.

"Now you must see what I can offer my loyal followers. I can give you a share in the dominion of the earth. I need you, lieutenant. Name your price, and you shall have it when the earth is under my heel—even if it is a whole nation."

Hall shook his yellow head.

"No, Renvic," he said flatly. A swift anger made him blurt, dangerously: "You don't need me, Renvic. What you need is a strait-jacket."

Renvic flushed, and his hands made a furious clawing motion.

" 'All, you had better eat those words. Get down on your knees, and beg the forgiveness of Alexander. Or —die!"

Sick at heart, the American flier still managed to hold his head up defiantly. After all, nothing could now make things any blacker.

"Go ahead, Mr. Jones," he said. "Do your dirtiest!"

Anger expanded Renvic.

"Seize this man," he screamed. "Prepare for him to be shot at sunrise."

Jimmy Hall swayed, as hard fingers gripped his arms. He had been a fool, not to pretend to yield. But something in him rebelled at any duplicity. His defiance had succeeded in getting a good deal of amazing information out of Renvic. But probably he would not live to use it.

His numbed mind searching the future, Jimmy Hall could see only death. And death not for himself only, but for civilization. Even if Renvic should fail in the end, his attack would surely ignite the powder keg of an armed and war-primed world.

His heart lifted a little, however, when the gray motorcycle came roaring down the road from the castle, and its reckless rider turned out to be Linda Gaylord. She wore a jaunty yellow sweater, that modeled her high proud breasts. Rest had restored all her red-haired beauty. Still he couldn't believe her a complete accomplice of Renvic's. But she greeted the pale man with a dazzling smile.

"Alec!" she shouted. "Your fugitive is found! One of the Mongol spies has just ridden in to claim the reward."

Hall was forgotten.

"Found?" echoed Renvic. "Where?"

"In some canyon off in the bad lands northwest. There is a spring and the ruins of an old monastery. The spy watched from the cliffs. He swears he saw her there. He says she's with a white man."

"I'm going after her," barked Renvic. "Krošeć, get a plane ready."

Meantime, the gray eyes of Linda Gaylord found Jimmy Hall, standing between his guards. Her lovely face looked puzzled, as:

"Jimmy," she demanded quickly, "what's the trouble?"

"Trouble enough," Hall muttered. Then his voice went ragged with an urgency of pleading. "Linda, you got me into this. Won't you—can't you help me out?"

"I made some promises," she agreed. "I'll speak to Alexander."

Beyond Hall's hearing, she slipped a smooth arm through Renvic's. He saw Renvic's angry glance at him, saw the cruel set of the thin pale face. Then the girl flushed suddenly. And at last she came back to Hall, white and quivering with scornful anger.

"Well, Mr. Secret Agent," her cold voice flayed him, "I've got to admit you were pretty good. You had me going."

He saw the tiny quiver of her lip. "Fortunately, Alexander was a little harder to deceive."

Her trembling hand made him a little mocking gesture of farewell.

"An operative of your acuity will understand that there can be no appeal from the necessary rule that spies must die."

Hall's big body jerked forward, against the hands that held him.

"Linda!" he gasped hoarsely. "You can't believe that!"

"I do."

"Then," his low voice croaked, "I know what you are. You are Renvic's—"

She ran away from him. In an instant she was on the motorcycle, thundering ahead of a plume of yellow dust, back toward Renvic's castle.

CHAPTER IX

The Man Who Crawled

A SPY! Through the hot afternoon, as Jimmy Hall paced wearily back and forth behind the barred iron door of his cell in the sandstone guardhouse, that began to seem like a very good idea.

Obviously, Renvic had turned Linda against him by telling her that he was an agent employed by some outside power. Hall was shaken with a cold hatred of the girl—she was doubtless hoping to share Renvic's world dominion.

But certainly the world had need of a good secret agent here, to stop Renvic or carry warning out. It was not a job that Jimmy Hall was trained for. He could see no considerable hope of achieving either aim.

But he grimly resolved to try.

The chance of escape seemed small enough. Most of Renvic's men must be adventurers in the worst sense, itching to share the loot of the world. Cupidity, as well as fear of Renvic, would hold them loyal. There was the G-ray projector, standing guard over the camp. There was the ray of cold. And the desert's stark hostility would be another barrier.

Small hope enough — but it was all there was.

Hall peered out through the grille in the heavy steel door. A gray clad sentry carried a rifle back and forth outside. The tower that carried the silver egg of the G-ray projector stood a hundred yards away, on the plateau's edge.

Clearly, he would have to wait for darkness.

The strange jewel, the little winged golden figure on its ruby chain, was the key he planned to use. He was glad there had been no time to bring about its return to Renvic.

Darkness fell at last. A motor generator began drumming somewhere. Lights flashed out, through the camp. Great floods burned down from the tower. Hall heard automobile engines, saw men moving about. He imagined that some unusual excitement filled the camp, wondered if it had anything to do with the mysterious fugitive after whom Renvic had gone.

No enlightenment came. At last, tired of waiting for quiet, Hall decided to make the attempt. At first the guard ignored his shouts. Hall was beginning to think the swarthy fellow knew no English. But at last he changed his beat, so that he walked nearer the door.

"I can make you a millionaire," Hall's cautious voice assured him. "You have heard of the jewels that come in the plane? Well, I have one of them. If you want it—unlock the door and give me five minutes."

"Zat so, buddy?" Hall instantly guessed that his guard had once been employed at some cheap lunch counter in America. "Where ze jool?"

Stepping well back from the door, under the single unshaded electric, Hall let it dangle from his fingers. Blood-red rays lanced from the ruby chain, golden breasts gleamed, and the bright wings glittered enticingly.

The guard's dark face was a grimace of triumph.

"Thanks, buddy," he snarled. "Now jes' geeve it over."

"Open the door," Hall said. "And give me five minutes. If you hold me up, I'll tell your officers you have it."

"Geeve it!" The guard leered at him. "Or I'll shoot—and say you were attempting to escape."

Hall's plan of operations had included that. The heavy little figure swung on its chain, in his quick fingers, as the guard leveled his rifle. The two crashes were close together. Hall fell, with the fragments of the light globe. He groaned, attempted a death-rattle, and held his breath.

A long moment of agonized waiting —then he heard the lock.

He lay quite still, until shoe leather grated on the stone floor beside him, until the smoke from the gun barrel stung his nostrils. When the muzzle prodded his body, he seized it, twisted, struck.

With a muted cry, the guard went down.

Hall reversed the rifle, replaced the useful trinket in his pocket, and ran to the door. He had hoped to slip out quietly—hoped even for some miracle of good fortune that would set him aboard one of the big gray planes.

But evidently the gun-shot had caused alarm. A shouting officer came at a run from the line of tents, with half a dozen men in gray behind him.

This was no time for halfway measures. The rifle was a Mauser, with four shots left in the vertical box. From inside the doorway, Hall emptied it. The officer went down with a broken leg. Two men fell. The rest wavered. Hall dropped the gun, and sprinted for the plateau's rim.

THE wounded officer screamed commands to his men. Lead ricocheted and shrieked about Hall. But aim, as he had just learned, was uncertain by artificial light. Twelve seconds from the guardhouse, he plunged down a ragged talus slope into darkness.

He had most greatly feared the great silver egg of the G-ray projector. But perhaps the operator of that was absent or napping. For the lofty case did not move.

Hall at first ran in great desperate strides down the black slope, trusting the mental map he had made of the canyon from the air, that day.

For haste was obviously imperative. Sirens wailed behind him. Presently a great searchlight thrust its glaring eye over the rim. Now and then a rifle twanged, once a machine gun coughed briefly.

In his youth, near his father's mission, Jimmy Hall had known country much like this—where growing ravines had devoured the farm lands. Often he had played bandits-and-caravans in them with the native boys.

Now he played that old game again, with death for a penalty. And, it might be, even the safety of the world as the prize. All the old skill came back, as he crouched in narrow crevices, climbed silently down banks of splintered shale, slipped across dry, ever-deeper gulches.

The G-ray, at last, went into action. For a clay pinnacle above him gleamed out abruptly in the darkness, as if illuminated by a spotlight of ghastly purple. And then it crumbled, flattened as if a great invisible hammer had crushed it. No dust, even, rose against that awful force.

After that, he clung to the black canyon bottoms.

It was a G-bomb, from which he had the closest call.

An airplane was roaring in the sky. A Verey flare had floated down ahead, vanished. And the bomb struck, without other warning, some distance up the slope.

The thud of its fall was just audible. There was a sudden flare of dull purple light, that was somehow searingly painful to his eyes. And he was flung down upon his face, as if his weight had been several-fold increased.

His hands and face were lacerated by the fall. For a few seconds he was pinned against the gravel, unable even to breathe. But, with the fading of that dull, blinding purple, the burden of weight departed.

Hall squeezed his bruised body against a boulder, until the plane had dropped another Verey flare, and dived to see the bomb's effect. It roared over, and left him. He rose again, and staggered on.

He was anxious to get as far as possible, before dawn. His stumbling progress was slow by starlight. After midnight, however, the gibbous moon picked out the larger obstacles, and he held a steady pace down the main, deepening canyon.

In the dawn, when motors began to roar again in the sky, he found the shelter of a shallow cave. He slept through the morning, presently awoke to the torture of thirst. At dark, reeling now with hunger, he went on.

All that night, slogging wearily down the canyon, he hoped to come upon some seep or rainpool. But the dry desert mocked him. And it came to him, with a horrible certainty, that in the land itself Renvic had chosen a better guard for his secrets than all his gray minions and the terror of the G-ray.

For this day would surely bring madness.

The next night, Hall thought, would be his last.

In that stupor of fatigue and despair, plodding through the chill gray of dawn, Hall heard some hoarse, croaking sound. A thing came to meet him, crawling up the dry gravel stream-bed in the bottom of the canyon. He saw at last, with a shock of incredulous horror, that the thing was human.

The man moved in a manner a little ludicrous, more than a little frightful. Holding his wrists close together, he made a queer hopping step with his arms. Then he lurched his body, to drag his knees forward.

The stranger's body was bare to the waist. The sun had cooked his back to a hot brick red. His close-trimmed beard was black, but the hair on his head was completely white.

The crawling man came up on his lacerated knees. The hands he held up, close together, were worn bloody paws. In a moment, Hall saw why he held them together. The swollen, bleeding wrists were cruelly bound with wire.

His ankles, Hall saw, were likewise tied.

A harsh, rattling sound came from the throat of the red-eyed stranger. And the big pilot shuddered to a thrill of deeper, puzzled horror. For that dreadful croaking made his own name: "Jim! Jim Hall!"

CHAPTER X

Conqueror to Come

HIS steps stiffened with dread, Hall walked slowly up to the kneeling man. He searched the thin, pain-drawn face beneath that tangle of white hair. For all the black beard, the inflamed eyes, the cracked and swollen lips, he glimpsed some ghost of the past.

"Don't you know me, Jim?" It was hard to understand the dry, agonized croaking. "Don't you remember Randolph Field? The kid from Boston? The one they called Beans?"

"Boyd?" Hall was incredulous. "Carter—you aren't Carter Boyd?"

"All that is left of him."

"What — in God's name, Carter — what has happened to you?"

But Carter Boyd didn't hear him. He had pitched suddenly forward, on his face. Hall attacked the wires. They had been twisted mercilessly tight, with pliers, and then cut short, so that naked fingers could do nothing with them.

Thrusting the blade of his pocket knife between the twisted ends of wire, Hall was able to loosen them. When Boyd was free, he dragged him into the shadow of a cliff, and rubbed at his swollen wrists and ankles to restore circulation.

After an hour, Boyd came to.

"Thanks," he croaked. "Sorry I passed out, old man. But I had been going all night. Knew it was my last chance."

"You'll be all right, old scout," murmured Hall. That is, he held back the reservation, if we don't die of thirst before Renvic gets us with his G-bombs. "Now—if you can stand to talk—who did it?"

Horror shadowed Boyd's dark eyes.

"I don't know." His pale face twitched with pain. "It was a green-eyed devil in black, with a gang of men in gray uniforms. They came in a queer gray plane, and took her away."

Sobs shook Boyd's red-burned shoulders.

"They took Shadrona, and carried her away!"

Green-eyed devil! That fitted Renvic. Breathless, Hall dropped to his knees on the gravel, beside Boyd.

"Shadrona?" he demanded. "Who's Shadrona?"

The dark, blood-shot eyes of Boyd stared up at him. They looked almost insane.

"Shadrona's an angel. We were in love. Those devils carried her away."

"An angel? What do you mean?"

Boyd's white head dropped wearily back to the gravel.

"I can't tell you, Jim," he whispered. "Don't think I'm out of my head, Jim. I'm as sane as any man ever was. But if I told you about Shadrona, you would know I was crazy."

"You've got to tell me, Beans," Hall urged him hoarsely. "We're both in a pretty bad pickle. We've got to work together."

Boyd shook his white head, wearily.

"You wouldn't believe, Jim. Even I couldn't believe in Shadrona at first. If you did believe, you couldn't understand—not how a man could love a winged thing—"

"Winged thing?" Hall caught at the phrase. He fumbled in his pocket. "Carter," he asked softly, "would it help you to tell me about Shadrona if I showed you—this?"

He produced the strange jewel. Light glittered yellow on the slim nude woman-body hung from the ruby chain, shimmered from the many-colored wings.

"Shadrona!" Boyd almost screamed. "It is Shadrona!"

His stiff bloody hand reached quivering, and Hall let him have the jewel. His reddened, hollowed eyes studied it. At last his head shook.

"No, it isn't Shadrona," he gasped. "But where did it come from, Jim?"

"I don't know," Hall said. "But now, Carter—can't you tell me?"

In short, gasping phrases, Carter

Boyd told of the freezing music and how he had fought the gray planes, to aid Shadrona. How she in turn had saved his life, carried him to the valley of the ancient monastery, nursed his wound.

"And Renvic found you?" Hall prompted him.

"The gray plane came," Boyd's dry, tortured voice doggedly continued. "I didn't think any plane could land in that narrow canyon—but it did.

"I tried to get Shadrona to escape. But she wouldn't leave me. She tried to defend us with her weapon of cold. But a queer purple ray smashed us down—"

"The G-ray," muttered Hall. "But go on."

"When I came to," gasped Boyd, "they had us. The green-eyed one was standing by, snapping orders. A big, black-haired devil had the wire and pliers."

HALL'S whisper hissed through clenched teeth, "Krošeć!"

"They called him that," husked Boyd. "He had tied the joints of Shadrona's wings together behind her back. He tied her feet. His black face wore a look of ghoulish delight. And I couldn't endure the way his big, savage hands—"

Boyd bit his blackened lips. Blood oozed down, into the black beard on his chin.

"I tried to fight," he went on at last. "That — Krošeć clubbed me with his gun. His men held me. He tied my wrists and ankles with the wire. Then he fastened my arms up to the branch of an old apple tree, so that I was half hanging.

"Shadrona was just coming back to consciousness. The wires must have been agonizing. For she made little whimpering sounds, that would have torn your heart out.

"Panting with a beastly passion, Krošeć crushed her in his arms.

"Then he began to laugh. 'We'll leave your friend to hang there,' he told her, 'till his bones fall apart.' He carried her into the plane. One of his men picked up the cold-weapon, and they took off."

Pity choked Hall.

"How—Carter—how'd you ever get away?"

"It was an old tree, Jim. The branch was dead. I managed to break it with my weight. Then I tried all day to untie the wires. I failed. When night came, I started to crawl.

"Once I had thought I glimpsed a Mongol horseman up on the rim. I hoped to find a camp—"

"The spy!" whispered Hall, "who found you!"

"That night, I crawled," gasped Boyd. "The next day. And last night. Till I met you." His dark, tortured eyes stared at Hall. "Now—what can we do?"

"We've got to stop Renvic." Hall's voice was hoarse and grim. "He calls himself Alexander. He is going to attack the world, with those weird weapons. He'll try to conquer civilization, if he isn't stopped. And the odds are about a million to one, against us."

"But we've got to try," sobbed Boyd. "For Shadrona."

"For the world," gasped Hall's dry throat. "But first—water!"

CHAPTER XI

DWELLERS IN THE SKY

AS IF Renvic had decided to leave Hall's fate to the merciless hands of the desert, they saw no searching planes that day. Staggering,

Hall aiding Boyd, they went back the way that Boyd had come.

Beyond a welter of tumbled boulders which it seemed incredible to Hall that the crawling man could have crossed, they found a well-concealed rift in the age-shattered canyon wall, and came into the tiny green valley of the lost monastery.

Laughing with a kind of delirious joy, they drank.

That same day, Hall prepared to leave again.

"We've got to have more information," he said, "about what we're up against. And I think I know how to get it."

Carter Boyd insisted that he must go along—until his haggard white head fell in exhausted sleep. He looked obviously unfit for any effort for several days. Taking a little food and a pottery jar of water, Hall left him sleeping.

Venturing now to travel by day, Hall was able to move more rapidly. But it was late on the following day when he glimpsed the ominous silver tower that guarded the plateau's rim.

His plan was a desperate gamble. Its basis was no more than a pit and a spade that he had glimpsed from the air, and chance words that he had overheard. The armed sentry, stalking back and forth on the rim above, made the attempt seem wholly foolhardy.

At last, giddy with hunger and fatigue, Hall reached the pit unobserved. He secreted himself twenty yards below it, and waited for Dr. Gaylord—cold with a sudden doubt that the archeologist would ever return to his dig.

But at last, just before sunset, the little scientist came waddling eagerly down the trail. The monocle glittered beneath his white pith helmet. An automatic was belted over his shorts.

He hurried down into the pit, and went to work. The end of some huge gray bone was projecting from the red clay. He was uncovering it with careful skill. He used a chisel to pry off bits of clay, removed the fragments with a tiny brush, and covered the huge ancient bone, as fast as it was exposed, with shellac.

He made a tuneless buzzing sound as he worked.

Hall came up silently behind. He caught the butt of the automatic, removed it. Still Gaylord buzzed, unconscious of him. Hall set the muzzle against his stooped back, and said:

"Sorry, Doc, but I've got to interrupt."

The little man emitted a startled howl. His chisel gouged deep into the gray brittle bone. His monocle fell out of his eye, shattered. White and trembling, he blinked at Hall.

"I won't hurt you, Doc. I've just got some questions to ask."

Swelling angrily, Gaylord pushed the topi back off his red bald head. He pointed at the deep gouge in the bone.

"Look what you m-m-made me do!" his thin voice shrilled. "I know what you are. You are a secret agent in the pay of the German government. Renvic told me. I'll not t-t-t-tell you anything."

"We'll see."

Gaylord's moon face froze into a stubborn frown.

"I won't b-b-betray Renvic and his Plan."

Hall jabbed him sharply with the gun.

"Better, Doc." His voice was a menacing rasp. "All about Renvic and his Plan and the winged people and whatever place you found them. Quick!"

The small eyes of Gaylord narrowed cunningly.

"Not a word about the Rock!"

For answer, Hall caught up the dropped chisel. He drove it into the buried bone. Soft fragments splintered out. And Gaylord made a little scream of pain.

"Don't do that! You'll destroy my *Cycloptosaurus Gaylordi* — the only specimen — my chance for immortality!" His fat hands groped vainly at the chisel. "D-d-don't!"

Hall lifted the chisel grimly.

"Talk!"

"All right," sighed the little man. "For the sake of science, I will tell you. Only, put down that chisel!"

HALL obeyed, but kept the automatic level. Gaylord fished another monocle out of the pocket of his red polo shirt, and inflated his chest importantly.

"As you would be aware, young man, if you read the scientific abstracts, my genius has been displayed in many fields of research. It was an investigation of the Cosmic Rays, three years ago, that led to the discovery of the Rock."

Hall was a little surprised at his sudden willingness to talk. Was there a catch to it?

"I was making high altitude flights," Gaylord went on, "carrying Geiger counters and a portable cloud chamber of my own design. Count Renvic was my pilot."

"Renvic?" Hall broke in. "Who was he?"

"My daughter met him at a party in Hollywood. He was then a penniless refugee. With his Iron Shirts, he had attempted a revolution in his own country. They were defeated and exiled. He and Linda were attracted. She persuaded me to employ him."

"Now," said Hall. "About the Rock?"

The little man was peering through the monocle, up toward the plateau's rim. His face set stubbornly. When Hall reached for the chisel again, however, he resumed nervously:

"Descending through a cloud, we struck the Rock quite by accident. Renvic managed to level off, but there was damage to both ourselves and the plane."

Amazed, Hall demanded:

"What is the Rock?"

Gaylord cleared his throat.

"The Rock, as my unpublished monograph shows, is a stone mass of igneous origin, nearly four miles in length, and about one thousand feet in extreme thickness. It floats on the atmosphere, at an altitude of about three miles."

"Floats?" rapped Hall. "How?"

"By an almost complete nullification of gravity," said the shrill-voiced little scientist. "We haven't got the full secret, yet—that's why Renvic was so anxious to recapture the fugitive.

"But, like the gravity-multiplying G-ray, it depends upon the mass-velocity relation. Weight is increased by acceleration of electronic spins. The nullification, from the evidence at hand, seems to follow the same principle. The spin, however, is apparently on a hyper-axis, resulting in a minimization of the time-factor."

"If there's a Rock floating in the sky," demanded Hall, "why hasn't it been seen?"

The monocle glittered superciliously.

"The surrounding atmosphere," squeaked Gaylord, "through an extension of the anti-gravity effect, is lightened, so that a continual up-current rises about the Rock. The resulting rarefication, cooling, and condensation surrounds the Rock with clouds and mist. That condition has caused it to be mistaken for a more or less ordinary atmospheric disturbance."

"Well," Hall muttered. "And what did you find on the Rock?"

"The Rock is covered with snow," Gaylord said. "In the center of it stands a singular city. The buildings are cylindrical and crowned with flat, disk-shaped platforms. There are no streets, and few ground-level doors. For the inhabitants are—or were—a unique race of winged avian mammals.

"They were highly intelligent. It seems a misfortune for the science of biology that Renvic found it necessary to kill so many of them before a proper study had been made."

Hall's lean face was grim.

"How did he come to kill them?"

"They were extremely friendly, on the occasion of our first landing," the little scientist told him. "They cared for our injuries, and helped repair the plane. The trouble developed when we returned with a larger expedition.

"While I was carrying on scientific observations, Renvic set up a trading post near their city. Previously, we had seen the wealth of these beings— at some earlier period in their history, they must have worked extensive mines on the surface of the planet. They had flying machines, that once had been used in that commerce—we discovered several useful aerodynamic principles from a study of them. Their early visits, by the way, doubtless established the Icarus legend, and the various myths of winged supernatural beings.

"At any rate, Renvic brought a plane-load of glass beads, bright calico, cheap Japanese-made trinkets, whisky, and opium. Unfortunately, however, difficulties developed at the trading post.

"THE winged beings refused to drink the whisky or use the narcotics, or to buy the other merchandise. There was some charge that Renvic and his men had seized and violated a young female.

"Finally, a delegation of the rulers demanded that we leave the Rock. That, of course, threatened my scientific research. But Renvic met the sit-

uation. At first I objected to his plan. But he pointed out that these beings were, after all, only animals.

"We detained the delegates, and offered to release them in exchange for certain advantages—it was thus that we learned the secret of the G-effect.

"Still, however, Renvic suspected opposition. On the day when our prisoners were to be released, he gave a feast to which the entire population was invited, as a sign of our new friendship.

"We had discovered that these beings, while disdaining alcohol, would accept sweetened soda-water. Scores of them came to our camp. They appeared totally innocent. But Renvic suspected some plot.

"Cleverly, he had put large quantities of opium, lead acetate, and arsenic into the refreshments. Those who refused to drink were destroyed with machine guns. Captain Krošeć led a band of men into the city, to forestall any counter measures.

"Only one of the creatures, in the end, was preserved alive. That was a young female, who seems to have been some sort of attendant at a pyramid-shaped temple. We hoped to question her, but she unfortunately escaped, with a heat-absorbing weapon.

"Recently, however, she has been recaptured, and taken back to the Rock. Renvic informs me that in the interim she has learned English. He is confident that she will soon be forced to give up the information we require. He is already building a more powerful model of her cold-ray."

Hall's face was gray and tense. Hoarsely, he asked:

"Where is the Rock?"

The monocle glittered cunningly.

"It d-d-drifts about. One day it is here, another there."

"But you have a way of finding it?"

Gaylord shrugged.

"Another thing," rapped Hall.

"Where is Linda?"

"She accompanied Renvic to the Rock."

A slow but furious anger had risen in the breast of Jimmy Hall. He tried to control it, enough to speak reasonably. For he must appeal to Gaylord's humanity, seek his aid.

"Look here, Doc, do you believe those beings were justly treated?"

"They were not human, as Renvic explained," squeaked the little scientist. "Therefore, justice did not enter. Our only considerations were expediency and the advancement of science."

"Don't you understand," quivered Hall, "that you have been aiding the greatest criminal of history? That Renvic is planning to attack the world—"

Across his voice cut Gaylord's thin, triumphant scream:

"Men, seize this spy!"

Hall felt the shadow over him. In one sick instant, he realized that his absorbed interest in the story of the Rock had dulled his caution. He knew that Renvic's men had come down from the plateau, while Gaylord talked; perhaps called by some covert signal.

His smouldering anger found one expression. He drove the chisel into the shellacked end of the great bone, shattered it to gray dust.

Then, as gravel grated under a thrusting foot behind him, he crouched, tried to turn. But a savage blow, from somewhere behind, caught his head. He toppled into darkness.

CHAPTER XII

The Rock in the Mist

NIGHT had fallen, when Jimmy Hall recovered consciousness in the same sandstone cell from which he had previously escaped. Now,

however, he had four guards instead of one. And the strange jewel, which once had brought him freedom, was gone.

It was a bitter night. The guards ignored his hoarse requests for water. Despair haunted him. Exhaustion dragged him back to the stone floor. He slept in snatches. But his head ached, under blood-matted hair, where the blow had struck. Thirst tortured him. He could not forget bloody-kneed Carter Boyd, and lonely Shadrona, whom he had failed.

The dawn came at last, with only new despair.

For little Gaylord came waddling to the door of the cell, and glared through his monocle, squeaking:

"Lieutenant Hall, you had better make yourself ready to die. I reported your capture to Renvic. He has radioed an order for you to be shot. I will give you an hour."

"Wait, Dr. Gaylord." Hall clung to the bars. "Don't you realize—that will be murder?"

The monocle glittered coldly.

"I might overlook the evidence of the stolen jewel, found on your person," shrilled Gaylord. "I might ignore Duval's testimony. But your wanton destruction of my *Cycloptosaurus Gaylordi* convinces me that you are fundamentally undesirable."

"I'm sorry I did it, Doctor," gasped Hall. "I was just so angry—"

"You've one hour," Gaylord cut in sharply. "That is Alexander's order. There will be no appeal and no escape."

The bow-legged little man stalked away and left him.

Hopelessly, Hall stalked about the cell. So far as he could see, there was really going to be no appeal and no escape. The gigantic stone blocks of the walls were impregnable. The four guards ignored even his croaking demands for water.

Presently he leaned weakly against the door, staring vacantly through the bars. On its lofty tower, the silver egg of the G-ray projector glittered in the sunlight. Beyond, the bad lands became a glare of dull hot color.

With only a weary interest, he saw gray-clad men running. He heard sharp commands, shouts of alarm. A siren wailed. Then a great plane roared over the building. It came down into view before him—diving for the G-ray tower!

Breathlessly with a new, incredulous hope, he stared.

A gray wing caught the projector's bright case, flung it off the twisted tower, and down out of sight into the canyon beyond. The great bomber, spinning aside from the impact, also dropped out of sight.

Hall was certain it had been wrecked. He was wondering what desperate airman had sacrificed his life to destroy the weird weapon—when the battered plane came roaring back up out of the canyon! One wing half crumpled, it still flew.

It limped out of his sight, toward the landing field. Five minutes later, Renvic's gray-armored limousine pitched to a stop, with screaming brakes, in front of the guardhouse. A group of the gray-clad Balkan officers, white-faced, tumbled frantically out. They barked commands at the guard, and the door of Hall's cell grated open.

"Come, lieutenant!" one of them called. "Queekly!"

But Hall, supposing this to be the firing squad, showed no haste.

"Queekly!" The officer ran to seize his arm. "It ees the lady in the plane —the Mees Gaylord! She has a G-bomb! She threatens to destroy the whole camp—unless we breeng you queekly."

The incredible fact burst upon Hall. It was Linda Gaylord whose reckless dive had destroyed the G-ray machine!

He tumbled into the car. It went roaring back to the flying field. The battered gray plane was standing in the middle of it. Beside the plane, a slim defiant figure, stood Linda Gaylord. Her red hair was disheveled from some struggle. The yellow sweater was torn, exposing half of a swelling white breast. Upended beside her was the tapered bright cylinder of the bomb. Her hand was evidently on the fuse.

She motioned the car, at some distance, to stop.

THE officers pushed Hall out. He started running toward her, reeling with hunger and thirst and fatigue.

"Jimmy?" Her clear voice was sharp, desperate. "You're all right? Then get one of the other planes—I ruined this one. Be sure it's fueled. And come by after me. Hurry! I'll hold 'em till you're ready."

Her voice pealed out again, as Hall turned. It crackled, in the native tongue of the Balkan officers. Whatever she said, it made them jump to Hall's aid.

In ten minutes, one of the big gray bombers was ready to fly. Hall taxied it out toward where the girl waited. She motioned for him to get out. He helped her lift the deadly bright cylinder into the cabin.

"Now call one of the officers," she said. "I've got some word to leave."

Hall beckoned, and a frightened man in gray came running to the plane. Speechless, he turned white as he listened. The girl finished in English:

"That's it. Tell the others. Don't touch a plane. I'll give you fifteen minutes to get out of the way on foot. Then we're going to drop this G-bomb!"

The officer turned, shouting. His words started a frantic exodus from the city of tents. Desperate men in gray scattered toward the surrounding canyons. The red-haired girl smiled triumphantly at Hall.

"All right, Jimmy," she shouted. "Let's go!"

But Hall waited. For he saw a ragged, sunburned figure stumbling toward the plane at a limping run, recognized the bare white head of Carter Boyd.

"A friend of mine," he told the girl. "We'll need him. And what about your father?"

"Don't worry about Dad. He's already flying to Hong Kong, with a plane load of his old bones."

Haggard and gasping for breath, Carter Boyd tumbled into the cabin, fastened the door. Hall gunned the big plane across the field, roared over the suddenly emptied city of tents, climbed.

Boyd stumbled forward.

"Why did you leave me, Jim?" he asked hoarsely.

Hall glanced at his swollen, blood-stained wrists.

"You weren't fit—"

Boyd's dark, deep-sunken, blood-shot eyes burned resentfully.

"You know I'm fit," he declared, "to help Shadrona! But I thought I'd never overtake you. All day and all night—"

Turning suddenly white, he slumped down weakly.

When they were eighteen thousand feet above the plateau, so high that buildings and tents and big gray bombers were turned to toys, Linda Gaylord rolled the G-bomb's heavy cylinder into a slot in the floor of the cabin. She did something to the fuse, and motioned Hall to dive and release it from the cockpit controls.

The bright fleck of it vanished beneath them. The purple flare glowed small and briefly, close to the guard-house. The instant collapse of tents and buildings and planes was visible, even from their elevation. And Hall knew that the plateau no longer carried any menace to the peace of the world.

Now there was only that other, more secure stronghold of Renvic's, upon the flying Rock. But how, he wondered, could they hope to tackle that—

Linda came swaying forward. Now that this crisis was passed, all her cool self-possession had deserted her. She was trembling, laughing, crying. She collaped in the seat beside him.

"Please, Jimmy!" she sobbed, "won't you forgive me? I've been an awful idiot. I guess I was—well—" her face blushed scarlet— "sort of infatuated with Renvic. But thank God that's over!

"He made me believe that a gang of German spies were trying to get the Rock and its treasure and its secrets, for the Nazis. He made me believe that he was making all his own military preparations, just to stop the Nazis from conquering the world—and that you were one of their spies.

"Can you ever forgive me, Jimmy?"

Hall's tired hollow face grinned at her.

"Seeing what you've just done, darling, it looks like I'll have to! If you'll just hand me the water canteen and a bag of sandwiches I made them put in the plane." She held the canteen, and he drank. "How come," he demanded, "this sudden change of heart?"

"Shadrona told me," she said.

THAT name jerked Carter Boyd out of what had seemed unconsciousness. He pulled himself up, gasping:

"Shadrona—where is she?"

"Give him a drink." Hall passed back the water. But Boyd held the canteen in his quivering hands, waiting for Linda to speak.

"She's on the Rock," Linda said. "She wouldn't tell Renvic what he wanted to know. Krošeć almost killed her." Horror shook her voice. "I went in the hospital hut, to nurse her. She had pretended to be unable to speak much English. But when we were alone, when she saw that I was sympathetic, she talked to me.

"She told me what Krošeć and Renvic had done to her. She told me things she had heard them say—that revealed their real plan of world conquest.

"She cried, and clung to me with her little golden feet that are so much like hands. It was terrible, Jimmy. Renvic had always spoken of her as just a queer, intelligent animal. But she's—human. Her eyes were human. Her sobs, so terribly human!

"She made me realize what Dad and I had helped Renvic do. And I promised to help her escape. There was someone she wanted to go to. A man, I think, named Boyd."

The white-haired man made a gulping, breathless sound.

"But Krošeć overheard. He reported to Renvic. Renvic came storming out of his own hut, his green eyes terrible with anger—I don't know how I ever imagined I loved such a horrible devil!

"I had to leave Shadrona. But I managed to get to a plane that had just landed, and took off into the mist. They couldn't follow, because it's so cold on the Rock that you have to heat the oil in a motor before you can start it. So I got away.

"It happened that the plane had a G-bomb aboard. I told the men at base that I was ready to set it off—even if it killed me, too. And you know what happened."

Jimmy Hall put his big arm around her trembling shoulders. He left the big plane fly itself for half a minute, while he crushed her against him. He covered her responding hot lips with thirsty kisses.

"I know," he whispered at last. "And now what?"

"Shadrona!" It was a dry-voiced, desperate gasp from Carter Boyd. "We've got to get to Shadrona."

Linda's red head nodded, against Hall's big shoulder.

"That's right," she said. "Now Renvic knows how well she can talk. He and Krošeć will torture her again. If they get the secrets they want, it will be too late even to hope. Renvic will have the earth in the palm of his hand!"

"Shadrona!" The white-haired man was sobbing like a child. "Shadrona—tortured!"

"Linda," Hall asked, "you can find the Rock?"

She nodded. "Just keep on east."

"But after we get there—what?" His voice was grave with apprehension. "I gathered up a few rifles and automatics. But, against those weapons of Renvic's—" He shuddered. "There isn't another G-bomb?"

"No," she said. "Renvic didn't trust his men too far. Most of his weapons are on the Rock. The bomb I used was the one you refused to drop, Jimmy."

"Then," Hall demanded wearily, "what can we hope to do?"

"There's one chance," the girl said. "If we can glide in silently through the mist, and land unobserved, we may be able to surprise them. But if we are discovered—if they catch us with the G-ray—or with that new freezing beam—"

Her lovely face was pale with dread.

"I know Renvic—at last, I do. He's the stuff of dictators. Half genius, half lunatic. Now he'll be furious and a little frightened and utterly desperate. We could never have won, back at camp, if Renvic or Krošeć had been there. On the Rock, it will be a different story."

Holding an altitude that made the surface a gray blur beneath, they flew on eastward. From time to time, Linda gave Hall brief directions. Once she tried the radio.

"They have a beam station on the Rock," she said. "But it's off, now—they must be on guard. But I think I can find it, anyhow."

Food and water refreshed them all. The girl and Boyd relieved Hall for a while at the controls. Hour after hour, the big plane thundered on. The Siberian coast fell behind, and the warlike islands of Japan. They were over the vast Pacific.

"There!" whispered Linda, at last. "The Rock!"

But Jimmy Hall could see nothing unusual about the balloon of white vapor, brooding above the gray ocean. It looked like a common thunder cloud. A blue streak of rain fell beneath it. Jagged lightning stabbed down, now and then.

"Climb!" the girl said tersely. "So we can glide down into it with the motors silent."

"But, darling, it's only a cloud—"

Hall's protest dropped into a gulf of amazement. For a momentary rift in the veiling vapor revealed the strangest vista he had ever looked upon.

CHAPTER XIII

DEATH IS A WEARY LOAD

PARTED like a curtain, the high white clouds revealed a fantastic landscape.

Adrift in the mist was a bit of irregular plain, snowswept, broken here and there with dark projecting rocks. Little gray huts were clustered in a camp on the snow, beside a line of huge gray bombers.

Beyond, upon a low hill, stood a city. It was an incredible fairy city, taken from the dream of a child. The tall cylindrical buildings were striped with vivid color. Each was crowned with a flat flying stage. There were many high windows, with recessed balconies, and few openings at the level of the ground.

"Shadrona!" Carter Boyd gasped hoarsely. "Her city—"

"Down!" Linda's voice was cold with apprehension. "Or we'll be seen!"

Hall tipped the bomber down. In a moment that eldritch cloud-land vista had closed. He climbed again, and presently cut the motors, set the big ship in a long glide down into the clouds.

His heart was thumping hard. He half expected a gray-winged armada to burst out of the white vapor ahead. He shuddered from the anticipation of some deadly beam, that might hurl them toward the far sea.

But there was no attack—perhaps, after all, they had not been seen.

They plowed into the mist. Ghostly wraiths scudded by them. Linda spoke tense-voiced directions. And at last, so close his breath caught, Hall made out a rugged, snowy slope.

He pulled hard up on the wheel, released the braking flaps. The landing wheels struck a rock, bounded. Twisting metal screamed. The big ship whirled. For one cold instant, Hall thought they were going back over the rim. But a snow bank stopped them, ten yards short of falling.

Mopping sudden sweat from his face, Hall looked at the girl.

"Well, we're here!"

Linda smiled back, uncertainly, and squeezed his arm.

"The city's a mile away," she whispered. "Their camp is beyond. We can slip through the rocks. If there has been no alarm—"

"Shadrona!" gasped Carter Boyd. "We must get to her."

"Do you know where the G-bombs are kept?" Hall demanded. "If we could get into the arsenal first. Or perhaps divide forces—"

With brief words, the girl sketched out the way ahead. The men stumbled out, ahead of her, into the snow. Bitter cold stung their skin. The thin air took Hall's breath. But he caught Linda, crushed hasty fevered kisses against her face and her white throat.

Then she screamed a warning. He had released her, to fumble in the cabin for the weapons, when the G-ray struck them.

From the direction of that fantastic city, an orb of searing, blinding purple burned dull and sinister in the mist. The sudden, colossal weight of his body crushed Jimmy Hall down into the snow. And he felt a new deadly bitterness of cold.

He fell against the big plane's intact wheel, in a half sitting position. That terrible eye continued to leer out of the gray, drifting mist. Ice-crystals made weird circles around it. And the awful pressure held him fast.

He could hardly breathe. He couldn't even lift his hands. He couldn't turn his head, against the wheel, to see what had become of Carter Boyd.

But Linda Gaylord lay within his line of vision. She had fallen headlong backward, and now she lay motionless, pressed deep into the snow. That terrible weight of multiplied gravity molded her clothing against every slim curve of her limbs and her waist and her proud breasts. Flung back over her head, her hair was flattened against the snow like a red fan.

All hope deserted Jimmy Hall. Every breath, against the terrific weight upon his chest, took a desperate effort. He sensed an eerie, silent vibration, and knew that this ray carried the stolen power of Shadrona's cold-weapon. He shivered, and then a dull numbness sank into him.

A slow ache grew in his chest. His vision blurred. He knew that his heart, laboring under this terrible burden, couldn't long stand the strain. He could see no possible hope. He began to wish that Renvic would step up the power of the ray, and make a quicker job of it.

FOR a long time he thought that Linda was unconscious. He knew that she still lived, for he could see the labored rise and fall of her breasts. He could hear her tortured breathing. At last her voice came to him, in terrible forced gasps:

"Sorry, Jimmy. Want—to say I—love you!"

Hall tried to fill his big chest, choked out two words:

"Check, darling!"

Then he saw the men coming. A dozen of them, plodding on snowshoes. He wondered why the purple G-ray did not pin them down, why the radiant cold did not congeal them. Then he saw that each of them wore a bulky, hooded suit of some dark thick fabric —obviously, a sort of radiation-armor that shielded them from the ray.

The G-bombs, even if he could have got them, might have been useless after all.

The group paused, at some little distance. Hall recognized, despite their bulky suits, the two who came forward alone. Bull-like Krošeć, and green-eyed Renvic!

Krošeć stopped. His black-gloved hand rested on the butt of an automatic in a thick black holster.

"Ach!" he snarled. "Verdammt Americain Schweinhund—who iss now what you call der dog-on-top?"

Pinned fast, Hall could only glare back at him.

A satanic laugh echoed hollowly from the hooded head of Renvic. He came to the side of the girl. Kicking off the snowshoes, he drove his black boot roughly against her side.

The girl made a choked, whimpering sob.

"So you tried to betray me?" whipped out the hard cruel voice. "You were going to release the winged creature?"

His boot came down savagely, upon the soft curves of her breast. She sobbed again, piteously.

Hall had thought himself quite unable to move. But Linda's cry did something to him. A red fury blazed, giving him a strength he had never owned before. Every fibre of his body fighting the awful gravitation, he dragged himself upward.

He forced his hands up, against that appalling pressure. He caught the bottom of the cabin door. Slowly, his muscles snapping, he pulled himself up beside the plane. He reached into the cabin, and felt the butt of one of the rifles.

Darkness was pressing on him, as it did when he pulled a plane out of a dive too sharply — because the blood was drawn from his brain. His body was stiff with the cold of the ray. And a cold sickness of despair fell back upon him. For the rifle was riveted to the floor, by that terrible gravity. He couldn't move it.

Slumping against the plane, he turned again.

Renvic had now fallen on his knees beside the helpless, prostrate girl. His black-gloved hands were ripping off her torn yellow sweater and her riding breeches. He tore away silk undergarments. Her white loveliness lay naked in the snow, crowned with her hair's red fan.

Goose-pimples appeared on her smooth skin. It was already blue with cold. So exposed to the wind and the ray, Hall knew, she could live only a few minutes. But, from the agonized rise and fall of her full white breasts, he knew that she still breathed.

"So you turned against me?" Mad violence clotted the hard tones of Renvic, as his lecherous black fingers stripped away the last shreds of clinging silk. "You dared defy me — the Alexander!

"Well, now you weel pay for all you 'ave done, here in the sight of your lover." His satyr's breath was panting. "Pay for all you denied me, for all the years you 'ave put me off. And then you die!"

A flurry of snow swirled across her fair nudity. Thick cold blood spread slow stains, where Renvic's fingers or his boots had scratched her shivering body.

She made a little choked sob.

Her muted cry gave Hall strength to move again. He lurched forward, empty-handed. It took a savage effort to lift each foot. His pulse was a hammering in his ears. A burden of darkness pressed upon him.

Krošeć was staring avidly at the girl. It was Renvic—now a green-eyed devil indeed, as unveiled evil passion moved him—who looked up from the naked girl and shouted:

"Kill him, Krošeć—if you want her when I am done!"

"*Ach, ja!*" boomed Krošeć. "I keel him!"

The hairy man, gigantic indeed in the insulating suit, came lumbering toward Hall. The American stood swaying, helpless—it took all his strength just to keep erect.

Krošeć pulled his automatic out of its holster. The gun must suddenly have increased in weight, as it came out into the ray. For it seemed to jerk down, and Krošeć stumbled forward.

WITH a last prodigious effort, Hall plunged to meet him. Krošeć's terrific strength dragged the weapon up again. But Hall, simply yielding to that awful weight, fell against him. He wrapped his arms around Krošeć's bull neck, and dropped.

That fearful pressure did its work. The gun went off, into the snow. A deep harsh bellow of rage and pain came from Krošeć. And then it abruptly ceased. For Hall's arms, serving merely as a lever to apply that savage force, had snapped his vertebrae.

But that victory, Hall swiftly realized, meant nothing.

For the dead man lay across his legs. He knew that he would not be able to rise again, against that crushing weight. He scrabbled for the gun, but it was lost in the snow.

He saw Renvic rising over the girl's white quivering nudity, deliberately leveling a huge automatic. Then it seemed to Hall's failing senses that the purple, right-ringed orb winked malevolently in the mist. He felt another wave of that piercing, deadly cold.

And darkness crashed upon him.

CHAPTER XIV

THE FALL OF SHAR

CARTER BOYD, when he clambered out of the half-wrecked plane, stumbled over a snow-covered rock. Chance pitched him out upon the deadly slide, that they had all escaped so narrowly. A minor avalanche gathered about him, bore him swiftly down.

Staring into the up-swirling mist, he realized suddenly that there was nothing at the bottom of the slope—nothing but three sheer miles of vacant space, and then the far Pacific!

Desperately, he scrambled for safety. He reached snow that was not moving. Trembling with relief, he watched a white fall break over the awful brink beneath him.

Then the G-ray burned through the mist.

He was far out of its center. But its effect was still enough to start all the snow about him, in a greater slide. Frantically, staggering under the burden of his sudden weight, he stumbled across the moving snow.

He slipped, fell, was swept down with it.

Just at the brink, however, a point of black rock split the river of snow. He struggled toward it, snatched for it as he passed. Sharp rocks tore his fingers. But he managed to pull himself up upon it. For a little time he clung there, with the rumbling slide flying into a white spray about his feet.

When the avalanche had ceased, he made a perilous way back up the bare slope. He came at last to the level again, some distance from the plane. Now outside the freezing purple ray, he could see that Hall and Linda were pinned helpless in it.

There was no direct aid, he knew, that he could give.

After a moment, he set out, alone and weaponless, toward the center of the Rock. The icy gray mist had thickened again. It hugged the bare, snow-banked slopes. His vision was limited to a hundred yards or so.

At last, laboring painfully for breath in the thin, icy air, he came within view of the fantastic towers of Shar. Circling the bright, cylindrical buildings, he cautiously approached Renvic's camp beyond.

Shadrona would be in the hospital hut. He located it, from Linda's directions—next to the one that flew Renvic's bizarre flag. A flurry of snow swirled out of the frigid beam, hid him.

Two sentries loomed ahead. He crouched against the wall, waited for them to turn. Then a silent rush carried him through an open door, into a darkened room. He closed the door, soundlessly, dropped a heavy bar into place.

As he started toward the inner room, where Shadrona should be, a male nurse met him. A bulky figure in white. Boyd leapt at him, tigerishly. His weight carried the man down, and Boyd heard a low, ominous sound, as his head struck the floor.

The man lay still.

Carter Boyd stumbled through the partition door, and came upon Shadrona. She lay on a white, narrow bed. Her slender golden body was covered only with her extended, shimmering pinions.

Her red-helmeted head lay back upon the pillow. Her eyes were closed, and she did not move as Boyd approached. He looked down at her. Her pointed golden face was tear-stained, drawn with pain.

He dropped beside the bed, kissed her lips. She stirred in her sleep. The bell-tones of her voice made a little muted murmur. She smiled a little.

Then he touched the velvety golden curve of her shoulder. That woke her. She shuddered from his touch, and screamed. When her great, slanted purple eyes came open, there was stark horror in them.

For a moment she stared up at him without recognition.

Then the horror changed to incredulous joy.

"Carter?" sobbed the bell-voice.

"I've come for you, my darling," whispered Boyd.

Bending, so that the fragrance of her was in his nostrils, he slipped his arms under her body, tried to lift her.

Only then did he discover the chains. Fastened about her slim golden ankles, and above the joints of the brilliant wings, they held her spread out, helpless, upon the bed. Hard steel jingled, as Boyd laid her back.

"Chains!" sobbed her sadly melodious voice. "Chains hold me. Till I tell Renvic secrets of Shar. Krošeć

whip me, burn me, twist me. Till I tell secrets of Shar." She shuddered. "Never I tell."

Boyd fumbled with the chains, helplessly. Padlocks held them cruelly tight. He heard shouts, outside. The barred door rattled.

HE ran back into the outer room, swiftly searched the groaning man in white. He found a bunch of keys. A warning bullet crashed through the door, as he returned to Shadrona.

The keys fitted. He lifted Shadrona into his arms. She clung to him, sobbing. Wildly, he stared about the bare, crude little room. His eyes searched for some weapon, some way of escape.

A fusillade of shots ripped through the outside door.

"What now, darling?" he whispered helplessly.

The warm silken softness of Shadrona moved in his arms.

"My pyramid!" pealed her clear bell-voice. "Secrets are there. Secrets I never told. There is fire of Shar. Fire that burns two million years. Fire that holds up Shar. Fire is fed with golden sticks, and lifts up Shar. We must put out fire."

Infinite sorrow throbbed in her tones.

"My people all dead. Need no fire."

Boyd stared down at her. Fire fed with gold—that must be atomic energy, maintaining whatever force held up the Rock!

"All right, darling!" he gasped. "And then what happens?"

"Put out fire," she sobbed. "And Shar must fall!"

Boyd's head lifted, grimly.

"So the Rock will fall!" he whispered. "Renvic and his devils on it! We, too, I suppose—but what does it matter? Let's go!"

He snatched up a little table from beside the bed, smashed a window out of the hut's rear wall. Shadrona scrambled nimbly through. He dragged himself after her.

Men came running around the building. There were guttural shouts, in an unfamiliar tongue. A rifle cracked.

But the soft limbs of Shadrona gripped Boyd's body. Her great wings spread. He ran a few steps across the snow, leapt. And they soared swiftly upward. Bullets hummed about them. But in a moment the low gray mist had curtained off their rising flight.

Jimmy Hall could never understand that instant of blind unconscious that fell upon him, after the terrible ray had already ceased. It was as if his tired heart, suddenly relieved of that appalling burden, had paused for a moment of rest. That uncanny deadly cold was gone, with the ray.

Renvic's gun was hammering, over Linda's supine nude body, when awareness flickered back. But the sudden return of the weapon to its normal weight must have caused Renvic unconsciously to thrust it upward.

For the shots went screaming over Hall's crumpled body, and off into the chill gray mist that swirled endlessly up about the rim of the Rock.

Crouching down behind the lifeless form of Krošeć, Hall dug frantically into the hard-packed snow for the automatic that Krošeć had dropped.

Before he had found it, however—and before Renvic's black-gloved fingers had finished snapping a fresh clip into his own gun, the American heard the terrible scream of the green-eyed man.

Looking up, Hall saw that something had caused Renvic to lose his balance. He had staggered up the steep, snow-clad slope below the half-wrecked plane —the slope that fell to the brink of the Rock.

It was swiftly, queerly, becoming steeper!

Renvic shrieked again. His nerve-less fingers dropped the gun. They clawed at the air. He fell, tumbled. Frantically, he snatched at a rock that he passed. But the thick dark radiation-armor made him clumsy. He missed it.

A final feral howl — more like the voice of a tortured wolf than a man's— floated back from that awful brink.

And Alexandrov Renvic was gone.

Hall turned back, toward the plane and the girl. Suddenly he was conscious of something very alarming. A steady, increasing push was driving him toward that deadly slope. Snow was beginning to slide.

The explanation came to him abruptly.

The whole Rock was tipping!

Falling, doubtless—though he didn't know why—into the Pacific.

Linda was sitting up in her bed of snow. She was pale and shuddering, and red scratches marred her body. But she was able to smile, very happily, at Jimmy Hall—before something made her turn suddenly from blue-white to pink, and cross her bare arms over her breasts.

Hall ran to her. It was like climbing a steep slope. His feet started snow-slides. But he reached her. Ignoring her gasp of surprise, he picked her up in his arms.

THE plane was already moving. Running back down the tipping surface, he just overtook it. He tumbled Linda through the open cabin door, scrambled after her. By the time he got the door fastened, the plane had slipped over the edge.

Stumbling forward with the shivering girl to the cockpit, he presently got one motor started, and then another, for they were not completely cold. The plane had been strained, by the G-ray as well as the crash, but it limped safely away from the falling Rock.

Looking back, Hall saw what happened.

The Rock fell out of the clouds that had so long veiled it from the eyes of man. It continued to tilt, and a rain of snow and debris fell from it into the Pacific. Hall thought he glimpsed some of the gray planes, falling—there would have been no time to warm them for flight.

Renvic's associates on the Rock must have perished, to the last man.

The descent of the Rock itself was oddly deliberate, as if whatever force sustained it had been very gradually withdrawn. At last, sidewise, it slipped very gently down into the gray Pacific. White foam glinted, and vanished. And then there was no mark left upon the sea.

Two hours later, Hall circled low over an American liner. When the damaged condition of the plane had been seen, and a boat lowered, he landed. The wreckage sank at once, but he kept Linda afloat until the boat reached them.

And so it came that they were sitting in a steamer chair one tropical night, staring back into the vessel's phosphorescent wake. The girl's vibrant body was warm in Hall's arms, and the fragrance of her hair filled his nostrils.

She shuddered, suddenly, and stopped his caresses.

"It's too bad," she whispered, "about your friend and Shadrona. They must have caused the falling of the Rock. It must have cost their lives."

Hall's arms squeezed tighter.

"I believe they escaped," he said. "Because I saw one plane that didn't fall. It was a queer machine, with wings that beat like a huge golden bird's. It climbed safely into the clouds.

"It must have been one of the flying machines that Shadrona's people used in the ancient times. I believe that she and Carter were aboard: I've got a mighty good hunch that they're all right —somewhere.

"Perhaps they are back in the old monastery. I don't know—I'll never know. Because I'm sure that they would rather be let alone."

"I suppose so." Linda Gaylord snuggled contentedly in his arms, and presently whispered, "I love you, Jimmy."

Hall grinned at the stars.

"Darling," he answered grimly, "you've told me so many lies—even if you thought the cause was good—that you'll have to spend the rest of your life convincing me of that. You can begin, right now."

Her warm lips lifted, and she obediently began.

The End.

I TALKED WITH GOD

(yes, I did—actually and literally)

LOVE'S LETHAL INGREDIENT

By ALLAN K. ECHOLS

Author of "Brides for the Damned," etc.

Here, then, in this half-world I would be eternally trapped, living only to witness forever a fiend from hell caress my lovely fiancee!

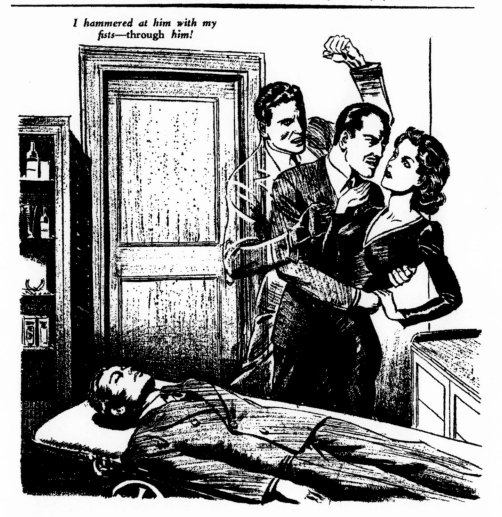

I hammered at him with my fists—through him!

I SUPPOSE I was fortunate in learning my lesson so soon. It cost me—God! What it cost!—but it was worth it. Now I might stand a chance of being as successful a man and a husband as I am a scientist.

I was glad to get back to my basement laboratory in the old brownstone house off Central Park and get to work; in a way I was even glad that my honeymoon was over. Not that I didn't love

Zelda with every beat of my heart—it was just that my experiment was so near to completion that I could scarcely wait to finish it. It would have offended her terribly if she had ever known at what inopportune times my mind reverted back to my scientific puzzle. Like that time she lay in my arms in the gondola in Venice, and the moon was a big gold wheel, and her warm breath fanned the tip of my ear and she

59

pleaded with me to hurry back to our hotel. . . . And I was thinking of my precious experiment! What a lover I was—*not!*

I guess I'd spent too many hard days and nights working. I couldn't have had much human impulse left in me, because on our first night at home I headed for the laboratory just as soon as dinner was over. Zelda looked at me peculiarly, but I didn't notice it at the time. She came with me to the laboratory door, and she had thrown on a sheer night gown with a negligee thrown over it. Her youthful figure was limned underneath these clinging garments as though painted with the brush of an artist.

She clung to me passionately, and I was not conscious for the moment of the longing she would not voice, for I suggested just a bit impatiently that she retire while I worked a while. I only knew that somehow her own feelings were being conveyed to me and tempting me to abandon the idea of working tonight, and this made me impatient.

"If you don't want to retire so early," I told her, "why don't you go out with your mother and Varden?"

Her only answer to that was to cling to me with her arms tighter around my neck and her lips burning into mine. "Please," she breathed, "don't work too long. I'll miss you so. . . ." And the look of love in her eyes again almost drove me away from my work for the evening.

God! If I had only been more red-blooded. If I had said, "To hell with the experiment," and left the laboratory for the evening. But I didn't, and, disappointed, she finally left me and I closed the door and turn to my bench.

I was all eagerness and trembling like a man who expects to be told that he has suddenly become the most important person in the world. I must have had visions of something almost like

that. The formula that I had been working on for so many years, and for which I had not found the proper amount of the final ingredient—this brain-child formula of mine was sealed in a rubber-stoppered retort, and I wasn't five minutes in getting it over a Bunsen burner and in bringing it to the temperature at which it would give off the vapor I wanted and would have—as soon as I found the proper proportion of that last ingredient.

I WAS standing before the work bench, watching the brown stuff as bubbles first began to form against the round bottom of the glass globe containing it. It was not very light in my laboratory in the basement of the old family home, but now in the yellow light of the single lamp that hung over my work bench I watched closely and saw the first tiny wisp of vapor curl up out of the neck of the retort.

This time I would succeed!

I was excited, and a little apprehensive, wondering whether or not the several weeks' time it had been standing while I was away would have affected it. So, as the first curling green wisp of vapor floated out of the neck of the retort, I leaned over the bench and placed my nose close to the mouth of it to smell it. The fumes drifted into my nostrils.

It seemed to smell the same—almost. I thought there was a small difference in the odor. But I did not have time to decide, for a heavy thud sounded on the floor behind me, as though a human body had fallen!

I turned around, startled that there should have been any one besides myself in the laboratory.

And then I gulped as I saw the body on the floor behind me. *It was my own body!*

I tell you, I was standing there over my own body, gazing at it in puzzled horror!

I stood there dumfounded and confused for a long moment, trying to convince myself that the crazy apparition would fade. I had a sense of rubbing my eyes, and the thought came to me that perhaps I was too tired, and had better not work so hard.

I tried kicking the body to see if the vision would fade, but it did not move. The body—*my* body—lay there on the floor, the features contorted with pain. I was lying there dead—and yet I was standing over my own body gazing at it! As the full meed of terror consumed me I began babbling something incoherent, trying to deny what I saw. But it would not be denied! My dead body lay on the floor at my feet.

I knew I had to get a grip on myself, to reason this thing out. I was always a methodical person, and believed that reason could explain anything. If it couldn't explain this thing I was likely to go raving mad.

I saw the mirror over my wash basin, and I crossed the room and stood before it, looking into the glass. I saw the other side of the room reflected in the glass—*but my own image was not there!*

I fought against the forces of panic that were invading my soul, but my reason was fighting a losing battle. I kept looking into that insane looking glass, trying to see my own reflection. But it wasn't there!

Maybe the trouble was with my eyes. I slapped my own face like a man patting on powder after shaving, and still there was nothing to see. The mirror said the room was empty!

Then I did cry out. Somebody must have taken the mirrored glass out and replaced it with plain glass. I reached out my hand to prove this was so.

Then I got my next shock! My hand went through the glass just as though there were no solid substance there.

Either the mirror had no substance—or I had not! And the mirror was there reflecting solid things, but not reflecting me. *Therefore I had no substance!*

I was gibbering like a lunatic as I turned and fled from that damned mirror and returned to where my body lay in front of my work bench. In the frenzy of my despair I hauled off and kicked at the body, as though it were the cause of my predicament. But my foot was like a shadow passing through a tree; it went right through without me feeling any resistance.

THEN I heard footsteps in the hall outside the laboratory, and my hopes were raised. I recognized the anxious voices of my wife's stepmother and her new husband, Doctor Varden. As remotely kin as they were to my wife, we were having them as houseguests to keep Zelda company while I buried myself in my work. I had never liked them, but now I thanked God that they were here. Doctor Varden was pounding on the door and shouting, "Are you all right?"

I shouted, "No. I'm not all right. Come here quickly, please!"

There was silence outside the door, followed by another knock. Doctor Varden repeated, "I say, are you all right in there? We heard a fall. Will you answer us?"

"I am answering you. For God's sake, come on in!"

There was another period of silence, then the doctor's voice. "That's strange, he doesn't answer. I wonder if we should take a chance on going in to have a look. I know he doesn't like to be disturbed—"

"Yes, I know," Mary Varden said, "but I think we'd better."

I felt a little relief as the doorknob turned and they came in. Mary Varden, Zelda's step-mother, who had married Varden after the death of Zelda's father, was still in her early forties and was pretty in a spectacular sort of way of which I didn't approve. But now I was glad to see her and her new husband. And I even thought of how glad I was that Zelda wasn't with them. The shock would have hurt her terribly.

Mrs. Varden took one look at my body on the floor, screamed and leaned weakly against the door she had closed behind her. Varden muttered something and rushed across the laboratory to the body.

I ran after him and tried to grasp him by the arm, shouting, "For God's sake, do something. I'm alive, but find out what that body is doing there and what's wrong with me. Hurry, will you!"

And then I had the feeling of my hopes being dashed to earth, and I knew the blackest despair. For I might just as well not have spoken! Varden neither saw nor heard me, nor felt my hand on his arm.

He knelt by the body and felt the pulse, and then opened one of the eyes and looked into it, paying no attention to my frantic shouts. My shouts and blows were not heard nor felt by him.

This thing that was the living me was not discernible to any human senses. Whatever of me this was which had become separated from my body, this part of me that could see and think and, yes, suffer the tortures of the damned, this part of me simply did not exist insofar as living persons were concerned. To them, that dead body of mine was all there was to me.

Doctor Varden looked up at his wife with a long significant look and shook his head sadly and said to her. "He's dead. You had better call Zelda and tell her."

"No," I shouted. "Don't let her know yet. There might be something that will—" But then came the realization that he couldn't hear me,

couldn't even be aware of my presence, and my words trailed off into a tortured sob.

Varden continued, "I'll go see her and break the news. You get a couple of the servants to remove the body to his bedroom."

Even knowing that my efforts were hopeless, I still followed him as he went out the laboratory door and up the dim hall, trying to clutch his arm, pleading with him not to tell Zelda yet. I even struck at him time after time, but my blows, my very fist made less impression on him than a breath of air.

I FOLLOWED him into our bedroom where he went without the courtesy of knocking on the door. Zelda was lying on the chaise lounge in her nightgown, and when Varden came in he stopped and I saw his eyes feasting on the loveliness of her which was reserved only for me to see. She got up and threw her dressing gown quickly about her lovely figure, and her eyes were burning with shame and rage.

As for myself I was cursing him roundly, and fruitlessly. I was clawing at him like a mad tiger—and he didn't even know it.

"Doctor Varden!" Zelda's face was flaming. "Why do you come in here without knocking?"

Varden interrupted quickly. He crossed the room and placed his hand on her elbow, which she withdrew. He said smoothly, "Listen, Zelda you have known all along what I have felt about you. I have loved you, and I still do. I want you to feel that I am your friend—"

"I wish you would go," Zelda answered hotly. "If it were known—"

"That's what I've come to tell you about," Varden answered. "You see, something has happened—"

Zelda's face blanched.

"—in the laboratory—"

My poor Zelda's violet eyes opened wide in fright as she looked at him, and then they were wide with terror as she read the truth in Varden's face.

She cried out in such fright that it tore at my very soul. I rushed to her side and tried to reassure her, tried to take her in my arms and comfort her, but even my own Zelda could not hear me nor feel my touch. I never knew that the torture of a soul could be as great as I felt at this moment. Here she was—

But she got quickly out of the room as she heard heavy footsteps in the hall. As she rushed out of our bedroom door I followed her. She was running down the hall in her bare feet behind the two servants who were carrying my body into my study, as a couple of men might carry an injured football player off the field.

Doctor Varden was already in the study when they laid my body down on the divan where I was accustomed to nap during my study periods. Zelda fell on the floor beside the couch and had my head between her hands, and a torrent of pleading words poured from her tortured soul as she kissed the cold lips of the body that lay there.

I think it was the sight of her own suffering that brought me to my senses and made me realize that I had been spending my time in a kind of panic instead of trying to do something. I realized that I had to act, had to do something more than to shout at people who couldn't hear me or even know of my presence.

Varden's hand was on Zelda's shoulder and he was trying to comfort her. I didn't like the unctuous way he did it, even under the guise of sympathy. "You've got to be brave," he said in an oily voice. "There's still a chance, perhaps. I'll call a doctor and the medical inspector. It seems, though, that you'd better be prepared for the worst.

But try to calm yourself. I'll take care of everything."

"Oh, what could have happened?" Zelda moaned. "How could he have died like this so suddenly?"

"There's always danger in a chemical laboratory," Doctor Varden answered. "Especially in work with strange and poisonous drugs. Of course you must have realized that when you married him."

THERE was a gloating look about the man's sensuous face that made me want to hammer him into a pulp, but my blows were meaningless to him. My rage was mounting as I realized that this man under my own roof was looking at my wife, even at a time like this, with the eyes of a lecher. I had never given such things a thought before, but now that it was too late, I was beginning to see things, to see that Zelda was a beautiful girl, that she was a human being who had expected love from her husband, and had got very little warmth in return, and that there were those who wanted the affection I had not brought myself to enjoy to the fullest. What a blind fool I had been. And how I hated this man!

I cried out in warning as he insisted on giving her a sedative. "Here, that's sodium amytal, and you're giving her an overdose," I shouted, but to no avail. Can you picture standing hopelessly by and seeing an overdose of drug being administered to your bride while you cannot even lift a hand to defend her? Hopelessly, I watched her close her eyes and sink into a deep slumber.

When he had seen that she was asleep, Varden went to the telephone to call our family physician. As I heard him report the accident and suggest that the doctor call the undertaker I went cold, and at last I realized that I had to make some effort to save Zelda and myself from the catastrophe that faced us.

My conscience was adding to my troubles for I felt that I had brought this upon us myself. God! Could she ever forgive me if she knew the truth? Could the sunshine ever come back into her beautiful face? Could her eyes ever light up again with that complete love with which they burned when I had taken her into my arms? Had I destroyed all this forever—all because I was curious to look into things that were forbidden man to know?

The Alchemists of the Middle Ages huddled in their dank cellars surrounded by their dried frogs and their blood and hair of slaughtered babies, and mixed these and other strange and forbidden things in their stinking cauldrons to the weird chants of their abracadabra in the dark of the moon. And they had brought forth their vile concoctions which they had called "elixir" and which they hoped would give the drinker thereof eternal life.

Perhaps they were half-mad, but they were the fathers of the modern scientists who today stand over their own cauldrons and continue the battle to defeat Death.

I was one of these scientists—a modern alchemist.

Briefly, the theory I was working on was a simple one, and I knew it was sound. Admitting that a living thing is composed of both a body and a separate entity which we may call life or consciousness or the soul, and that this thing called life cannot be killed, but merely isolated from the body it inhabits, admitting these things, it merely remained to separate the body from the soul. I believed that when that could be accomplished, a soul, if you will, which had gained long experience in this world and thus became valuable, could be taken from its wornout body and placed perhaps in a new body, such as, for instance, that of a baby which

had recently died. This new body would serve the old soul for another generation. Thus could be preserved the best and most fitting of mankind for generation after generation.

Thus, briefly, I had experimented. I knew I was right. I knew the experiment would be successful, and I should have already finished it, except for the hurried marriage of Zelda and myself.

WE had suddenly decided upon marriage on account of Zelda's stepmother. Neither of us had approved of her marrying Zelda's old father, who was ill at the time. We frankly considered her a fortune-hunting nurse. And we were even more displeased when a year after the death of Zelda's father, the new widow had married Doctor Varden, about whom nobody knew anything. I felt that Zelda's affairs were in danger some way, since her step-mother had Zelda's estate to administer as well as her own equity in the fortune of her late husband. So, Zelda and I were married, so that I could give her what protection I could.

Bitterly I now thought of how little protection I was affording her. But I had been too wrapped up in my laboratory work, and I was easily imposed upon.

Doctor Varden returned from telephoning. Zelda had fallen off into that drugged sleep which so frightened me. Now Varden picked her up, lifting her in his damned arms, I tell you, just as I might have done, and carried her off toward our bedroom.

I started to follow, but I stopped short when I saw that Mrs. Varden lingered behind. I saw a shrewd look on her face, just a furtive expression, but I didn't like it and I halted, watching her suspiciously. The thought flashed through my mind that here at least was one advantage of being invisible.

As Varden left my study, leaving the

woman and my dead body there, Mary Varden closed the hall door, then on swift feet she hurried to my private desk and threw it open. She rummaged through the pigeon holes, examining my private papers hastily and replacing them and looking for others. Then she found the one she wanted. I was standing just back of her, watching her, looking over her shoulder.

She had my will, which I had recently executed. She read it swiftly, together with the memorandum of instructions to be acted on in the event of my death.

I knew that she was disappointed, for Zelda's fortune was as large as my own, and I had arranged for my money to be used for scientific research, since Zelda didn't need it. I could see as she read that Mary Varden didn't like what she saw. She cursed softly in a very unladylike manner.

Then she tore the will into bits and put them into an envelope and burned them over an ash tray.

As criminal as was the intent of this action I at first could not figure out its significance. And then it dawned on me. If I died without a will my money would go to Zelda, and Mary Varden was the administrator of Zelda's estate. If Zelda died then—all her money and mine would go to the step-mother! *That was an amount of money worth committing murder for!*

I saw clearly that Zelda would be murdered! And I was helpless to prevent it now.

· The shock of the revelation drove me running squarely through the door, down the hall into our bedroom, driven by some futile urge to save her. I would have gladly spent a thousand eternities in hell for ten minutes of real, material existence in which to help her.

But I was to have no escape from the repeated shocks to my tortured soul. For as I ran into Zelda's room I stopped short, just as though I had been within my living body and found it paralyzed with a new, impotent rage.

There was Varden sitting on the side of the chaise lounge where Zelda lay unconscious. He had her head cradled in his arms, and he was shamelessly making love to her, drugged and unresisting and helpless as she was.

THE ghoul! The unspeakable loathing and hatred I felt for him knew no bounds, and my futile efforts to protect her drugged body from the caresses of his foul hands drove me to madness. Concerned not with the tragedy that had struck her, forgetful of her unconscious state, the man held her in his arms and talked to her as a ghoul might speak words of love to a corpse, as though his words could reach to her drug-clouded mind.

"I knew you were going to be mine sooner or later," he gloated. "And I could hardly wait. You hurt me with your indifference, and now you see what a mistake you made. If you had given me your love when I first asked for it this would not have happened to you. But you didn't. And this is what it has brought you."

I stood horrified, choked with a rage I couldn't put into action. Even so, I cried out, and threshed at him with my fists, at him and through him—and he didn't know it. But he would know it —if I had to haunt him until the Judgment Day! This I swore.

I saw Doctor Varden look up, listening, and then drop Zelda's body back on the lounge. And at the same time I heard the sound of new footsteps and the doorbell ring. Doctor Ruskin, our old family physician, had come at last. Maybe Ruskin could help me some way, if I could only let him know. My hopes arose a little and I followed Varden who stopped his lovemaking with a curse at the interruption.

In my study, Doctor Ruskin worked

over my body for half an hour while I stood by him and tried to communicate with him, but he finally shook his head. "It's no use, there's nothing that can be done." Then he asked: "Where is Zelda? There may be something I can do for her."

"You can!" I screamed in my voiceless fashion. "You can save her from being murdered—and worse. For God's sake, Doctor—"

But of course he did not hear me, and he was listening to Doctor Varden. "She has retired to her room. She was so overcome that I gave her a strong sedative which will keep her asleep until some of the shock wears off, poor girl."

"That's good," old Ruskin approved. "If you will look after her I will relieve you of all the necessary arrangements. I know that you all are broken up. Please see that Zelda is not present when the undertaker is here to embalm the body. I'll send him right away!"

The undertaker—embalm the body!

If it is possible for a being without a body to shiver, then the coldness which froze me at this new horror did that thing to me. This was a new peril I had not had time to think of. If they drew the blood out of my body and pumped arsenic into the veins, as the embalmer would do as soon as he got here, my last hope would be gone forever. I would be trapped in this halfworld, alone in the agony of my spirit, to live and yet not exist, to suffer this torture forever, for years and millions of years without end. At that moment I knew the full measure of the popular conception of hell!

It was punishment that it was past the endurance of man to contemplate, yet I would have resigned myself to it for one thing—the opportunity to save Zelda from being killed.

Satisfied that Zelda was properly cared for, kindly old Ruskin asked,

"Just how did the accident happen? I have always tried to caution him of the dangers of monkeying with unknown things."

"It must have been carelessness," Varden said sadly. "You know that he has been working on some problem which he never revealed. He went into his laboratory soon after dinner with the intention of working a short time. He couldn't wait till morning. Mrs. Varden and I happened to be near his closed door and we heard his body fall and went in to investigate. He was already dead. I saw the retort still over the fire and turned it off. There were the fumes of cyanide, if I recognized them correctly, and beside the retort on the bench there was an open bottle of cyanide tablets. In the notebook beside his work there were memoranda relative to the experiment and the use of cyanide in it. It seems clear that to me that he had put cyanide in the stuff in the retort, and that the fumes killed him accidentally."

UNSEEN to Varden, I stood aghast at his story. *"The liar! The liar!"* I fairly screamed with the charge, and I was jumping up and down, tearing at both the doctors as they talked, even though they did not know that I was doing it.

And then a great light dawned on me as the significance of Varden's statement clicked in my mind. And with it came a new ray of hope!

I turned and raced downstairs to my laboratory. Yes, there was the bottle of cyanide on the bench beside the retort, just as Varden had said he had found it.

I shouted to high heaven with a joy born of hope. Shouted now because I knew what had happened, because I knew for a certainty that I had been poisoned with cyanide fumes, I knew! I knew plenty!

I knew because I had not put that cyanide bottle there—*Doctor Varden had opened it and put it there after my body had been taken from the laboratory!*

Why? To make his story seem true. Right! Any autopsy would have shown that I had been poisoned with cyanide fumes. In that case, he had put the stuff into the mixture before I went to the laboratory. For I had *not* put cyanide into the mixture as yet!

Still, cyanide had gone into the mixture, and purely through a coincidence, the unbelievable had happened. He had intended to kill me, Varden had, but he had stumbled upon the precise amount needed to complete my formula —the amount I had been vainly searching for!

Instead of killing me, he had succeeded in solving my puzzle, and the stuff had done what I wanted it to do, detach the body from the soul! Keeping both intact.

Varden, having secretly seen my notes, and seen that cyanide was to be used, had used this knowledge for the purpose of completing the perfect crime.

I had been poisoned with cyanide, then. But I was still joyous, for there was something he had not known. And that was that the mixture contained other drugs that served to partially neutralize the poisonous effects of the cyanide and to produce still other effects. That was the object of my work.

Now I knew that I could do something to remedy the situation, for I hadn't been so foolish as to work with such drugs without also creating an antidote for it step by step. Thus as I had built up the elixir I had built up the antidote. It merely remained for me to add to the antidote for the rest of the mixture, the antidote for the added cyanide!

I could empty the cyanide bottle and see how many tablets were missing! But I had to work fast, for the embalmer would soon be here and then it would be too late.

I tried to do that—and I couldn't! For there wasn't enough substance to me to enable me to hold the bottle! My heart sank again.

But eternal death faced me. I *had* to find a solution!

And then I remembered my theory that this consciousness which was still alive must in the long run be some form of matter, perhaps made of a thin sprinkling of molecules. My theory seemed to have some evidence to support it, for even this disembodied part of me seemed to have form, the same as my material body had. If this was so, *I could prove it*—and save myself and Zelda!

I RUSHED over to a can of shellac in the laboratory and thrust my hands, my invisible hands into it, right through the tin. Again and again I bathed them in the gluelike stuff and then brought them out into the air to dry.

And then I gave a soundless shout of joy. There was some of the stuff sticking to the thin molecules which had the shape of my hands. It was working! I could see the dim, faint form of hands where mine should be, cloudlike, with their tiny amount of shellac which had stuck to the thin collection of molecules —but something!

Again and again I dipped my hands into the sticky stuff and let it dry, and slowly I began to see the dried coating on them, looking like a pair of animated rubber gloves moving in midair.

But they were now hands that could handle things—like the cyanide bottle. Working at top speed, I opened the bottle, counted the tablets and found seven were missing. I added the proper amount of ingredients for the antidote and filled a hypodermic syrings with it, and dashed up the stairs with it.

All that could have been seen, if anybody had met me in the hall, was a pair of rubber gloves rushing forward, one of them containing a loaded hypo. Fortunately I did not meet anybody.

But I stopped in my tracks in the hall when I heard angry voices coming from the Vardens' bedroom. I walked right through their closed door, found that the syringe and the shellacked hands would not pass through the wood, and compromised by just sticking my head into their room and listening to them.

Varden was lounging in a comfortable chair and his wife Mary was standing over him, talking angrily. She hurled her charges at him in a kind of frustrated rage as he sneered at her. "You want Zelda," the woman accused him. I've been watching you and you're not fooling me for a minute."

Varden smiled insolently. "Who's trying to fool you, my dear? She's a pretty little number, and I like variety. Understand?"

"Too well, you two-timing gigolo. And I'm not standing it for a minute."

Varden yawned in her face. "I'm afraid you're going to have to stand it, my dear. There's really nothing you can do to prevent it."

"Oh, isn't there? Suppose I tell the undertaker that you put cyanide in that bottle of goo he was working on before dinnertime? That you did it because you wanted his money in Zelda's hands, and that you wanted her, too, along with the money?"

"But you won't tell anybody those things, my dear. In the first place it was your idea to kill both of them. And then if you were to deny that, there is the mere detail that you overlooked getting a divorce from me the first time when you married Zelda's father. Which makes you a bigamist, and incidentally

a pauper and perhaps a convict. You wouldn't be able to keep a nickel of the money you got from the old man if the law knew that you were my wife when you married him. They might even look into the cause of his death—if you understand, my dear. And how would you like that?"

"You dirty—"

"Don't say it," Varden said casually. "I think I'll go across the hall and see how my little *patient* is doing. Would you like to see some *genuine* feminine charm? There's something about a young bride—"

I came to my senses quickly, for Varden was going to Zelda again. I knew all I needed to know. And now, if my antidote would work. . . .

In breathless eagerness I rushed down the hall and into my study, carrying my precious syringe of antidote. Would it work? Or should I fail Zelda in this last chance?

I stood over my own body, motionless a moment, fearful to face this last test. But it had to be done. To me the whole of existence depended on the result.

Then I plunged the needle into the arm of the body on the couch, and then into the other arm.

And it happened, more quickly than it takes to tell it. It wasn't startling, it wasn't even describable. It was simply that at one moment I was plunging the needle into the body that lay before me.

The next moment I was whole again, rising off the couch, as though I had been dozing for a moment. That was all. No forgetfulness of what had taken place; nothing except that I was again a complete living man. Otherwise I was the same as I always had been.

No, that is wrong. I was not the same. I was no longer the bookworm scientific student who had little contact with the world, a mouselike lover of peace. No, I was a man who loved a woman—and who had murder in his heart. I was a man hungry to kill a slinking creature who had betrayed me and the woman I loved. I was hungry for blood.

I got a gun out of my desk, my father's gun which I had never touched before, and tiptoed down the hall. I had to go softly now, for I could again make noise. And then I discovered Varden's supreme insult to Zelda and his own wife. *He hadn't even bothered to lock the door when he went into Zelda's room!*

It was as though he actually hoped Mary Varden would come and see him in his vile lovemaking!

I turned the doorknob, pistol in hand. And somehow there was exultation in me at the sight of him there, caressing my sleeping, drugged wife. I wanted to catch him like that, wanted to see him so as to fire my rage to greater flame. And it did!

He had his arms around her, caressing her with his murderous unclean hands. I stood framed in the door, gun leveled. And then I said:

"All right, Varden, are you ready to die?"

He whirled as though he had heard the voice of a ghost, and there was the light of madness in his eyes when he saw the man he thought he had killed standing before him.

He saw the gun in my hand, realized the futility of trying to do anything. And then all the cowardice that was deep in the soul of him flooded up in his being, and he sank to the floor, unable to stand in the weakness his fear had given him. He lay there and whimpered like a whipped cur.

I stood over him and begged him to stand up and take his punishment like a man, but it was not in him to do a thing like that, and he cried out in the torture of his fear. He wouldn't fight back.

I spat on him, and I knew that I was so contemptuous of him that I could not shoot him like I could have if he had been any part of a man.

Finally I said, "All right, get up, you scum, and come with me into your wife's room." I had to kick him in the ribs until he would get up and then he stumbled down the hall before me.

MARY VARDEN fainted when I threw the door open and marched her man into her room. I made Varden empty a pitcher of water on her, and when she returned to consciousness I gave her my orders sharply and without sympathy. I made her write a full confession of their plot and made both sign it. I made her write an instrument relinquishing her entire claim to any part of the estate left by Zelda's father, and a power of attorney for me to attend to all the necessary transactions restoring all rights in the property to Zelda.

I gave them the choice of prison or of disappearing forever—and instantly. I booted Varden down the steps as they left.

And then I went back and gave Zelda a hypo to offset the sedative Varden had given her. She opened her eyes and found herself in my arms. She looked at me for a moment with a puzzled expression and then said, "Why, I must have dropped off to sleep, and I had the most horrible dream—that you were dead—"

I put my hand over her mouth quickly. "Forget it," I told her. "I've got news for you. I finished my experiment—and it was a failure. I won't try it any more. From now on, you and I will just enjoy life, play games—"

"Kissing games?" she asked in a manner that made the suggestion seem to be the very thing I had in mind.

LUST RIDES THE

Fear of the Unknown was not so great in George Trant as foreboding that beyond the Border lust would be his mate!

CHAPTER I

YOUNG GEORGE TRANT was neither mystic nor necromancer, nor had he dabbled ever in any of their weird powers. Yet he had known, since he was a small boy, that he was not like other people. Strange vivid happenings, things which he might have done, but which he had not done, kept coming to him. Happenings, of which he had not been a part, yet, like the panoramic scene of a moving picture, he would see unfolding before his blank gaze. He saw it actually as though he were doing it.

BY RAY KING

Author of "I Share My Bride with Satan," etc.

He had never told anyone of this weird nameless thing that was within him. When he was younger and found out that it was not daydreaming, he was afraid he would be laughed at. As he grew older, he dreaded for people to look upon him as "different."

But the abnormality persisted. Always it puzzled and worried him; sometimes it frightened him.

None of this was in his mind, neverthelss, that evening as he stood in the small exotic studio of his mistress, Vivian Delmar, glowering at her.

"No use pulling that sob stuff on me again," he was saying. "I saw your sailor friend leaving this apartment last night after midnight. That's the third time I've caught you at double-crossing me. I've been a fool. But that's over with now—"

Vivian, with her violet eyes and drooping lashes and soft languorous body, came to him. She pushed back a chair and put her arms about his neck, her full firm bosom pressing hard against him, her red half open lips making their appeal. She said:

"Darling, you mustn't talk that way! Tacker just dropped in to say hello. He's rough and doesn't realize a lady can give orders and he must obey them. You know—"

Her slumbrous eyes cloyed to him. They were misty and passion laden; and her hot breath, fragrant, seemed like an evil furnace of desire, luring him, tempting him back into submission.

He tore her arms from about his neck. The hurt which lay in his eyes and the puzzlement suddenly vanished. He straightened and walked toward the hall, reaching for his hat and gloves.

"No, Vivian—I'm through. I'll send you the check for next month's rent and expenses. Let's not vituperate. No explanations or lies—they're not necessary. I've been played for a fool. We've defiled each other—I see it now. The whole thing has been pretty messy."

"Messy?" She was lighting a cigarette with trembling hands. She flashed him a furtive look as he paused

---

FANTASTIC FEATURE-LENGTH NOVELETTE OF OTHER-WORLD

ROLLER COASTER

"How silly you act," she said. "Calm yourself!"

at the doorway.

"Yes," he said. "You know. That thing I called love. God, how you must have laughed at me—such a young fool to be taken in so easily by you—"

"You got what you went after," she said bluntly. "Or didn't you?"

Her words made him pause. He came back into the room. Its fading twilight gave an air of mysterious memories. Again he remembered his burning desire for her. Had he thought at the time that it was love? Or had he pretended, even to himself, that it was love to hide the animal truth which lay behind his actions?

"Yes, I got what I went after," he said. "And you got what you went after: money. That's right, isn't it?"

He stood looking at her, ashamed that he had fallen so low that he must pay a woman and call it love. Pay her well, and then be double-crossed.

"You're very good-looking," she said. "You look much older than you act. What's come over you, George? You must have fallen for another dame. All this excitement over Tacker's visit—it's

---

OGRES AND THEIR PASSION-RULED PURGATORY!

---

not like you. Who's the dame?"

HE accepted a cigarette and a light. Somehow, it was difficult to go. Once out of here, and he would never return. Those long evenings—they had seemed so exciting when she danced for him, stripped to almost the last tiny transparent garment, and he had snatched her to him hungrily, devouring her with his hot lips and breathless passion—

"There's no other woman," he said. And then he wondered. Had Alice Lawson some vague influence on his present feeling of shame and resentment? But he brushed it aside. Alice was a slim fair girl of seventeen with wistful blue eyes and a piquant smile—half child and half woman. They had been children together. Then, for five years he hadn't seen her until yesterday. They had tea. They held hands. Her hand was soft and clinging and he had felt protective and superior.

The thought persisted. Had Alice made him see, as he looked into her lovely eyes, that his life was heading far away from the things she stood for? And had these things suddenly become important to him?

"No other woman?" Vivian said softly. She had linked her arm in his and drawn him to a nearby couch. She slouched back and drew him with her. He felt himself drawing inwardly away from her. What a schemer she was! A grim humor helped him see it all more clearly. He watched her now, without the fire of passion to blind him. Her hand smoothed his forehead; long languorous fingers; her smooth black hair, done in a knot at the nape of her swanlike neck, brushed his lips as she bent sidewise. It left him cold. But was he playing with fire!

He started to his feet; but Vivian clung to him. "You sit here, George. I'll get us a drink. Just one last drink together—our farewell, if you wish—"

It was easy enough to get into this kind of thing, but an ugly mess getting out of it. He felt like a combination of a cad, a weakling and a sucker. It wasn't a pleasant feeling. All his life, he'd been very much the he-man, timber-cruising in the north, polo-player of international fame, one of the youngest men to have a seat in Wall Street at the Exchange. Girls adored him and he loved them all. He'd never been a sneak, stealing up to apartments at night, creeping out before dawn, both for his reputation and the woman involved, until he met Vivian. But, for his mother's sake, with his international reputation as well as his wealth and social position, he could not chance a breath of scandal in this illicit love with Vivian. It had been galling. Vivian had a husband somewhere in the offing too, who might at any moment descend upon them to spite her desertion of him, so she said.

While her allure was irresistible, all this was strangled within him. But now it rose to face him in all its hideous truth.

Vivian had left him for the drinks. She now reappeared, turning on a faint pink light in the distant corner of the room. Its soft gleam showed him that she had changed into a filmy negligee. Her hair was down, its great long tresses falling in abandonment about her shoulders. Her eyes were bright, challenging him. God, what depths she was willing to go to retain her income from him.

"Our drinks," she said. She brought the dainty tray forward and placed it on a side table. He stood up, feeling suddenly self-conscious as he gazed at her filmy covering.

He had a sudden urge to tear it from her: to expose her in all her naked blatant assault upon his baser impulses, to strip her, to strike her. Suddenly his hand reached out: he tore at the garment, exposing her voluptuous coarseness.

"George—are you mad—"

"Why not let me tear it off? That's what you want, isn't it? You want to arouse me, get your grip on me again, don't you? Well, there you are. I'm looking at you. Last night it was Tacker. God, you've taught me so much—Let me get a good look—I want to remember you—I want to remember what a fool a man can make of himself over a woman's body—I want to remember that there's nothing sacred in your code—"

She was clinging to him now. There were tears in her purpling eyes. Her firm breasts pressed against his rough tweed jacket, as he struggled to release himself from her caressing hold. His hands got tangled in her hair. Its cloying, suggestive net infuriated him. Was it a fight against her or himself or both—

Her tears and pleas were smothering him. The room seemed suddenly small, stifling. And predominating, he saw this woman, acting: saw her coarseness, the sham of it all.

"Damn you," he muttered. "Let me get away from here. You—you living devil—"

THEN she unloosed her hold upon him. She stood back, like an animal at bay, surveying him, her expression changed miraculously, like a venomous evil caricature of the woman who had been there a moment before.

She spat out her words: "Go, you young fool. But don't think you'll ever be rid of me. I'll be with you, tormenting you, haunting you for the rest of your life. You'll never escape me. I've done something to you—those things I've done—"

But he did not wait to hear more. He rushed from the room, her threats vaguely, strangely terrifying him—

"You'll never escape me. I'll follow you to your death—pay you back, you'll see—"

Her words followed him to the elevator. Her high satirical laugh seemed to echo and stay with him as he was taken swiftly downward. Out in the darkened street, with its twinkling electric lights, he tried to steady himself. He must think of this episode as a dream, a nightmare. He must not let it become a living past, a true part of himself. It was over now.

But as he told himself that it was over, he shuddered involuntarily.

CHAPTER II

IT was nearly a year later when George Trant first saw the mysterious pallid woman. He was in an amusement park and he saw her as she stood among a group of people watching the embarking passengers on the roller coaster. Her aspect was so unusual that it caught his attention. He stared, at first casually, then with a breathless interest. The woman was tall and slender. Despite the sullen oppressive heat of this Fourth of July evening, she was dressed in black—a garment unrelieved by color save for a deep somber red flower which nestled beneath one breast. The black robe hung from her broad shoulders down her slim length to the ground. Over her sleek black hair a black wimple of gauze framed her pallid face.

It was her face that held him—a beautiful face, imperious, pallid beyond health, with the black frame of the wimple enhancing its whiteness. She was about ten feet away, partly behind him. He had turned, startled; and it seemed suddenly that he was staring into the dark pools of her eyes under the thinly etched lines of her brows.

Her lips, red as the somber flower at her breast, were sensuously parted.

After that farewell evening with Vivian, Trant had come to California and had not seen her again. He had heard she gave up the studio and left the city. But before his departure from New York, he saw Alice a few times. Then she went on a trip with her mother and he pulled up stakes and left while she was away. He was alone here in this small city, passing the Fourth of July in idleness. The gayety of the holiday night had made an unusual sense of loneliness come upon him, so that as he saw the pallid woman who seemed abruptly to be returning his stare, an impulse to join her rose in him.

He took a step toward her. But though he could not tell why, he only took that single step. It was as though a shudder swept him, stiffening his legs. The woman had not moved. Her face, impassive, held no expression. It could have been the mask of something dead. But her eyes were alive. They brooded upon him, as though, motionless, still they were latent with a sweep of movement.

Vaguely shivering, the husky young George Trant turned away and gave his attention to the roller coaster. The ticket window was beside him. Beyond it at the left, the little single seat cars were coming out of a tunnel, stopping to discharge the two passengers each of them carried. They came at intervals of perhaps a minute. Attendants shoved them to the right a few feet, where on a little tongue of the floor people were waiting to embark.

Impulsively Trant bought a ticket. It was years since he had been on a roller coaster. He shoved his way forward, joining the waiting passengers. Two for each car. Most of them were young, in couples. He saw that he might have to wait some time, because

whatever car he got would have to go with an empty place beside him, or with someone, also alone, whom he could join.

A few minutes passed. Then again he was aware of the pallid woman. Gaunt stalking figure, she had pressed forward. Queerly she seemed in the crowd, but not part of it. She was diagonally in front of Trant now. He found himself wondering how old she might be. Twenty? Thirty? Or a woman without age; just a gaunt, pallid, brooding beauty. Ignoring the crowd, she was threading her way so unobtrusively that no one seemed to notice her. No one but Trant. He could feel his heart pounding; and suddenly the vague impression swept him that he had seen this pallid woman before. Or had he? It was puzzling, because now she seemed quite familiar.

Abruptly Trant was aware that there was an empty car in front of him and that the woman was getting into it. Then he saw the attendants looking at him, and impulsively he pressed forward. And for just a second it seemed that the woman, seated now in the car, was staring at him. A gaze that was beckoning?

He took a few swift steps and reached the side of the little car. And in that second the feeling swept him that here was something momentous. Should he board this car, or not? Like a fork in the pathway of his life. An important choice of ways. A divergence, so that if he got into this little car now it would be taking another road, momentously different from the path into his future which he had been following.

That second of indecision was a weird chaos to Trant. It seemed, as he raised his foot to enter the car and join the pallid woman, as though within him there was a tremendous tumult of things at war. A wrenching of all his being. And with it, his heart was racing, pounding his blood, making his breath pant. . . .

THEN, over beyond the roller coaster in the crowd gathered there—with one of his feet already in the car—he thought he saw Alice, dainty cool, virginal in her plain white dress and light blue picture hat, gazing at him. He murmured to himself, "That looks like Alice—" He stared. She seemed to be walking toward him. She was closer now and he saw that it wasn't she. But it could have been: this girl had the same purity of contour in her features. . . . Strange. And his heart was not racing now—no pounding blood making his breath pant. But a faint vague longing. . . .

The blackness came so instantly that he was aware only of a cessation—a complete obliteration of all that was George Trant. Then he knew there was an interval; and he felt a renewal, as though again there was a George Trant, who was lying on something fairly hard, with a vague murmur of distant voices so muffled that he could distinguish only that they sounded human. But they were sharpening, clarifying. And the consciousness of his limp body grew until he was aware of his face, which was cold with dank sweat.

The roaring of his head was blurring the voices; and when he opened his eyes there was only a weird swimming blur with something white moving, focussing in a moment to be a young man in starched white linen who was bending over him.

"Well," the young man said. "What happened to you? Eat too much dinner? Do you faint like that very often?"

The husky young George Trant sat weakly up on the white couch in the Emergency Room of the Amusement Park; and he tried to grin.

"Did I faint? I guess—"

"You sure did. Just starting to board the roller coaster," the young doctor said, "and down you went. Out like a light." He put away his stethoscope, while Trant sat dizzily up and began to button his shirt.

"How silly of me," Trant said. "Never did that before, doc. My heart's all right, isn't it?"

"Right as could be. Nothing the matter with you at all, so far as I can see." The young doctor looked puzzled. "With a pulse steady and strong like that, what the devil kept you unconscious so long beats me."

Outside the small white room, Trant was aware of a distant commotion in the Amusement Park — the sound of running people, and shouts.

"What's that?" he demanded.

A Park Attendant loomed in the doorway. "Hey, doc—my God—"

They whispered together. "Better forget it," the attendant said.

"Sure," the doctor agreed. He came back to Trant. "Now you better rest a while," he said. "Then I'll call a car and have you taken home—our expense, you know. Unless you've got a car of your own here."

"What was the excitement outside?" Trant persisted.

"Nothing—nothing at all," the doctor said soothingly. "A drunk started a fight or something. They've thrown him out."

The Amusement Park sent Trant to his hotel. "How long was I unconscious?" it occurred to him to ask, as he left the young doctor.

"Oh, about ten minutes. What the devil made you stay out all that time is beyond me."

It was beyond Trant also. But an active young American hasn't much time for mysteries. Trant took a train that next morning for Seattle. And except for an occasional lugubrious memory of how he had apparently fainted for no reason at all, he forgot the incident. Memory of the weird pallid woman in black once or twice stirred his interest. But very queerly, somehow the memory of her was vague —so vague that he wondered if he really had seen such a woman at all. Or had he just imagined her?

That incident at the roller coaster was on the evening of July 4th, 1933. As it happened, on July 4th, 1939, again he found himself passing the evening— alone and somewhat lonely — in that same Amusement Park of the small California city.

Five years had changed George Trant very little. And seemingly it had changed the Amusement Park not at all, so that mid-evening found Trant passing the entrance to the roller coaster which obviously was doing business exactly as it had on that other Fourth of July evening just five years ago.

TRANT'S mind flashed back to how he had fainted here, just as he was about to take a ride. Whimsically it occurred to him to wonder if he would faint now. It was an idiotic thought. He hadn't fainted since, or anything like it. He bought a ticket. It was idiotic too, that now he found himself searching with a gaze of queerly mixed emotions, to see if the pallid woman were lurking here. Surprisingly, the memory of her was vivid in him now. He gazed around; but so far as he could determine, she certainly wasn't here this time.

Imagination can play tricks, even with a husky young American who is undoubtedly—so far as anyone can determine of himself—mentally and physically normal. It was imagination, of course, tricking Trant—his memory of that so similar time just five years

ago—so that now as he headed for the little tongue of board flooring, watching his chance to get an empty car, he found his heart pounding with the idiotic apprehension that he might faint.

But he shook it off; stood waiting among the group of merrymakers. Then he saw his chance. Here was an empty car, with no one to board it save himself. The attendants were holding it as he pressed forward.

He raised his foot to step into the little car. . . .

Certainly his consciousness recorded nothing like fainting. But he was clearly aware of a cessation—an instantaneous stoppage of everything. But this time instantly there was a renewal so that he seemed to feel that his existence had winked, as electric lights for an almost imperceptible interval, wink when the current is switched from one dynamo to another. It was as though, now, the throbbing thread of his conscious life had switched, with one motivating force cut off and another force instantly picking it up, so that he was aware now that the pallid woman was here in the car with him. She shifted her slender body on the narrow seat to make room.

An attendant lowered the swiveled iron guard-rail to their laps. The little car started. Hooks of a clanking chain caught it, and it began its creaking ascent up the steep incline. For a time Trant sat gazing down at the widening vista of the Amusement Park as its gaudy lights dropped away beneath him. He was conscious of the pallid woman sitting rigid, gazing straight ahead of her up the steep incline of the narrow wooden track with the clanking chain in its center that slowly was drawing them up.

At the top the little car, freed of the clutching chain, seemed to poise an instant as though gathering itself. Then it rolled forward, picking up speed, rounding a curve that pressed Trant sidewise against the pallid woman.

"Oh, I'm sorry," he said breathlessly. "Beautiful view from up here, isn't it?"

"Yes," she agreed. He was aware, though he did not look directly at her, that she had turned and was staring at him. "You came," she murmured. "I wanted you to come."

Ahead of them loomed a dip. The tiny car almost seemed to drop from under them, so that Trant for that moment had the feeling that he was weightless. Then the car seat pressed him as they hit the bottom and mounted the ascent.

"Wanted me to come?" he echoed. He turned to look at her as they swooped dizzily around a curve. Were they going too fast? The side rollers on the car pressed the insecure-looking guard-rail of the track, squealing with the pressure—so great a pressure that for a moment it seemed to Trant that the opposite side of the car would rise up.

The pallid woman gestured. "That guard-rail could so easily break—"

He saw now that her red lips were parted in a smile; her dark eyes burned on him. It seemed that her gaunt, pallidly beautiful face was smouldering with triumph. And the triumph was in her throbbing, vibrant voice:

"You're not afraid, are you?" she added. "That would be foolish. What has to be, will be, you know. You cannot change this road—now."

Afraid? He knew suddenly that he was most horribly afraid. The little car was going too fast—no question of it. They had topped the rise of that last dip with a speed that made Trant feel that the car surely must leap upward from the rails. And this woman. She seemed to him vaguely familiar. Had he known her sometime in the past?

"You cannot change it—now," the pallid woman repeated.

He did not answer as they plunged into a tunnel; and there was only the throbbing echo of her voice mingling with the roaring darkness. Trant clung to the bar guard-rail across his lap as he felt the car wildly plunging. Or was this only a normal ride—the normal exciting thrill of a roller coaster giving you the simulation of danger where none existed? The blackness of the tunnel seemed endless.

AND this woman beside him. Suddenly she seemed pulsing with haunting memories, luring him strangely, awakening memories, emotions which he had thought dead. Who was she? Whom did she remind him of?

Then it came upon him. It was Vivian—this pallid woman was in some indescribable way, the transfiguration of Vivian—as he had thought she was when first she lured him—as she herself no doubt had thought she was—the embodiment of exotic allure. And evil. The personification of evil, female allurement. He saw it in a rush of thought. A siren, gloating, dragging him down—down—

He swung to face her, as the darkness swept past them and the smothering blackness showed nothing save this hellish fiend by his side.

"You—you're Vivian—" he gasped. "That's it—you're Vivian—" Then he remembered Vivian's last threat!

The pallid woman's laugh was her only rejoinder. It was the laugh which had followed him from Vivian's apartment that night: the mocking laughter and menacing threats which somehow had made him know that this episode would never be dead, but would hang like a shroud about him, haunting him always. . . .

"Damn you!" he muttered. But the wind carried away his words. "I'll have done with all this—" He swung to face her. They were emerging from the tunnel. Or were they? It was lighter now. But he could not see the pallid woman. She was not there. She seemed to have faded away. Everything had faded save the rush of wind against his face and the rhythmic clattering of the track as the little car swayed and dashed forward.

Plunging to its doom. What a queer thought! The death of George Trant. The end of the road—this brief side-road into which he had turned, which was leading him now abruptly to his death. Like a ghastly premonition it swept upon Trant.

Clack-clack . . . clack-clack . . . the rhythmic song of the creaking wooden track seemed suddenly screaming: "You're going—to die . . . You're going —to die."

Crazy thoughts. Crazy premonition. He steadied himself as in the blackness of the tunnel he saw the little circle of light ahead—widening circle so that all in a moment its rim had flowed upward and to the sides and the car was out in the open again, still high up on the looped maze of scaffolding which held the winding, dipping track.

"When you saw me tonight," the pallid woman was saying, "when you stared at me that way, then I knew you would come." She had not gone. She was here beside him.

He gazed at her now as he had gazed, tonight, back there in the crowd. Her white face was so devoid of expression that it could have been the mask of something dead. But her eyes were alive—eyes restless with triumph.

"You're not afraid to die?" she was murmuring. "It has to be—now." Then suddenly as the wildly plunging little car leaped around a curve and he could only cling and stare numbly at her, she added:

"It's just on the next curve where the side rail of the track is weakened. You'll see we won't—quite get by it."

"No!" he gasped. "You're lying. You—*damned thing*—you're lying—"

He had shoved at the bar on his lap and was wildly trying to stand up. The car's plunging was dizzying now. To Trant all the world was a horrible phantasmagoria of swaying vistas of scaffolding — swaying vistas of colored lights down on the ground so far below.

"How silly you act," the pallid woman said. "Sit down. You'll only die just a little sooner if you fall out."

"You damned—thing," he gasped. "I know you now—you've tried to make me do a lot of things in my life. I guess I've always been struggling with you—"

He was c o n s c i o u s that he had dropped back into the seat beside her. This was to be the last curve. The car seemed going so fast that with horrible force it was pressing sidewise. A curve with a steep drop downward. He was almost sure that he saw the little board of the side-rail of the track which had weakened and broken loose. For hours doubtless it had been slowly breaking as each successive car pressed against it. But all the others had gotten safely by. Queer fate that made this car— now—the one that wouldn't get by.

Trant saw the end of his life coming. He saw it with just a numbed awe so that he sat stiff and tense with an abrupt calm wonderment as he faced Eternity which he knew was only a split-second away. He was vaguely aware of the crash—the grim splintering of the flimsy wooden track as the little car tore through it. And still more vaguely he was aware of a hurtling through emptiness—and the grim vague thud as he crashed and came to the End. The end of the Known.

The beginning of the Unknown. . . .

"Hey, what the devil's the matter

with you? Drunk?"

FOR young George Trant, again there was a blurred consciousness of a switch—like a great dynamo picking up an interrupted current.

"Come on, get out." He heard the park attendant's voice. He felt the attendant's hand under his armpit lifting him up in the little roller coaster car with its empty seat beside him.

"Eh? Oh, I'm all right," he mumbled.

He climbed out. Stood, dazed.

For a long time George Trant stood —that Fourth of July evening of 1939 —watching the busy roller coaster with its endless procession of cars. For a long time he stood wondering. Then suddenly he strode to an elderly uniformed attendant who was standing alone nearby.

"Haven't been here for five years, until tonight," Trant greeted with a smile. "I guess you've been here that long, officer?"

"Fourteen years last May," the old man said proudly.

"I was here July 4, 1933," Trant said. "You remember? Just about this time in the evening. Something— something happened here at this roller coaster that night five years ago. Remember?"

He spoke casually, but he was holding his breath.

"Ain't somethin' I'm supposed to talk about." The old man's voice instinctively lowered. "But you was here—"

"Yes. Right here at the roller coaster."

"Our only accident," the old man said. "Just about now—Fourth of July six years ago. The track must have broken—a car went through."

"And who—who got killed?" Trant murmured.

"Damned lucky thing," the old man said. "It just happened to be an empty car."

"Yes—that was lucky." Trant nodded abstractedly and moved away. And he was wondering. One may at least grope and wonder. The pallid woman? His own personification of some guiding force, within himself? Five years ago, here at the little roller coaster, he had come to a fork in the road of his life. Had it been the personifications of Vivian against Alice? Lust against purity and rightness of thought? Conceivably, it was the vision of a girl whom he thought at first to be Alice, which had held him from that ride; that fatal ride, which his body had almost taken— that was a might-have-been, perhaps, along and down the road of dark desire. Almost it had been destined to be a reality. And perhaps because of that nearness, something of him, five years ago, seemingly had gone on that ride. Was it his baser nature? And tonight, with a similarity of circumstance, he had been made aware of it.

What might have been! The awed Trant contemplated what a vast multiplicity of might-have-beens exist for everyone's life! What an amazing tangled web of branching roads we must tread! A million diverse pathways to a million-million possible futures for all of us! A myriad little separate turnings which stumblingly we must choose, most particularly if once we have allowed ourselves to be side-tracked from our given road. We are guided only by our capacity for the evil or the good within us. And all we can do is trudge ahead, clinging to what we think is the best road, with a maze of might-have-beens shadowy beside us.

Mysterious, awesome thing, this which we call life! Trant knew that he would always wonder at that weird vision of one of his might-have-beens— vision mysteriously given so that just for once he was allowed to gaze upon the Unknown.

MY BRIDE BELONGS

No, Greta Stard was no soulless scientist—she'd never have brought those lust-crazed aborigines back from the grave to woo me had she been that, she'd never have staked her greatest experiment on life!

As he charged I saw that he was wearing—Greta's dress!

CHAPTER I

GALATEA

I HAD been a bum, five years before, with nothing left to look forward to, when Greta Stard found me in Central Park one morning when she went for the constitutional that was as much a part of her life as breathing. I had slept the night in Central Park. I had slept several nights there—since it had been warm enough, in fact. I was grimy, dirty, empty of shame. Sometimes the world can do things like that to a man, especially to a sensitive man, a scientist not born to the rough things of life.

Often, in the five years that followed,

BY WHAT UNSPEAKABLE WIZARDRY WAS MARVIN TRASK ABLE TO

TO THE AGES

BY ARTHUR J. BURKS

Author of "Dance with My Bride and Die," etc.

I wished she had left me there, for what she did to me in those five years no other parcel of this thing we call life could have done. Oh, she wasn't a Jezebel, sucking me dry of emotion, nothing like that. She was worse. She was that utterly soulless thing, a woman who was not a woman at all, but a statue too beautiful to be the work of man, too empty of life to be the work of God.

In form she was divine. To see her was to go wild with desire for her. But to look into her eyes was to look upon a glacier and feel the coldness of its winds across one's flesh.

She looked down at me, with contempt on her lips, in her eyes.

"You are, or have been, a scientist," she accused. "You might have been a good one. Why aren't you, and what is your name?"

"I was a scientist," I said, "and a good one. I'm not because I loved a woman. She did me dirt and I couldn't take it, nor forget it. My name is Marvin Trask."

Her eyes widened, ever so little. "Marvin Trask?" she repeated. "The man who, at twenty-five, produced a living thing from its ingredients?"

"Yes. Now, who are you?" I had risen to my feet, conscious for the first time that my feet showed through my shoes.

"Greta Stard. I'm something of a scientist myself. Just now I'm working on something of vast importance to the human race. You might, if there is anything left in you worth considering, help me out."

"What's the experiment?"

"Proof that man is really all his fore-bears. I use myself in my experiments, but when I do that I am unable to record the results. I need a subject, one preferably who doesn't care what happens to him."

"I take it there will be board and lodging with the job?"

"Yes. And money. All strictly business."

I grinned at her. I couldn't fancy a woman picking a bum out of the park on strictly business. There had to be an angle to it. I knew women, or at least one woman, and this one . . .

"I mean it," she said coldly. "Get all ideas out of your head you will ever be my lover. I have no time or patience with adolescence. Well?"

"Lead me to it," I said. But she had thrown me a challenge, without intending to, interesting me in a woman for the first time since my own hellish debacle. I had a yearning for just such a woman as this—a professedly unattainable woman.

That began it. I was enthralled by her laboratory, high in a penthouse on Park Avenue. It had everything in it that money could buy. The place possessed Greta Stard. In it she was more a machine than ever—and one of the finest minds I had ever encountered. Trouble was that she was so possessed by her science that she could never be a woman. I tried to find out about that, when we ended our first experiment together—an experiment in time traveling, since she hoped eventually to travel backward for converse with her own forebears, or with mine—by taking her roughly in my arms. The time was opportune, I thought, and the place all right.

WED NOT ONLY HIS BRIDE, BUT ALL HER ANCESTORS AS WELL!

It was in the middle of summer, and our experiment had filled the laboratory with undue warmth. For that reason both of us were stripped down to the barest essentials. I knew that with food and sleep I had become again the not inconsequential man I had been. And her scanty garments left nothing to the imagination. Knowing this, it was not strange that, in the heat of the exciting experiment, she discarded even the little she had worn.

LOVELY beyond all loveliness, she was. A black-haired Valkyrie, with a form beyond expressing in words. I caught her in my arms and kissed her savagely on lips that were red and full without the artistry of lipstick. And for a moment I thought she responded. She did, but only because I was part of her experiment, part of her triumph. She even strained against me. Then she remembered and pulled her head back.

"I told you, Trask," she said, "how I feel about this utterly silly thing men call sex. If it is necessary, in order for us to get along together—since I feel that your brain has become indispensable to me—let us have done with it as soon as possible!"

Some men might go for coldbloodedness like that; I had never been a great lover of statuary. I pushed her away. She forgot about it. Times and times, after that, she tortured me by appearing for work with no clothing on, knowing that I affected her no more than if I had been part of the furnishings of her laboratory. Nudity made her work easier, that was all. The same thing applied to me. It went on like that for five years, and I was as close to insanity as a man can come without stepping over the line. I was utterly mad about her. I might, if she had again offered, taken coldblooded submission, and asked for no more. But she did

not offer. If she had I'd have gone mad indeed, for even then she would have remained unattainable.

But even while I slept I could see her in the eyes of my mind. Shapely, curving hips, eyes as black as midnight, like her hair and brows and lashes. Breasts like mamay apples, newly ripe, skin like new rich wheat all mounded after the harvest. A mouth made for kisses. A mind that spurned all things emotional or physical. And I was still young enough to develop an inferiority complex about such matters.

Our latest experiment, though I could not foresee it then, was the straw that broke the back of the camel indeed. I won't go into detail. It is not necessary. She had discarded time travel as a way back to her forebears, on the theory that her forebears all lived within herself, and that by delving into her own subconscious she could contact them, become whichever one of them she wished. She had traced her ancestry back for fourteen generations.

There was a throne, in which she sat for this experiment. She had decided that I would do the recording of details of the experiment. Later, perhaps, I could go back in my turn. Just now, with electric wires attached to the arms of the chair, and a helmet on her head—exactly as though she were going to be electrocuted—Greta Stard was playing the star role.

"You are to watch me closely, as the current of electricity is increased. If I have done it properly, and I am sure I have, my subconscious will come to the fore almost at once—after I have gone into hypnosis. You are to release the current when this is evident, which means when I awaken as another person. You are to lead me out of the chair, away from the electrodes. You are to seat me in that chair yonder, and question me, recording everything I say —every last, solemn word, Trask! It is vastly important that I know!"

How can I ever forget that experiment? I stood back as Greta sat on the throne-chair so much like an electric chair, with her naked lovely arms on the arms of the chair, and told me in detail what I must do. I was, in effect, the "executioner." Her life was in my hands from the first coursing of current through her lovely, nude body. Her nudity no longer gave her pause for thought, so unimportant was I to her as a man. She didn't even know when she wore clothing, when she didn't.

Her body writhed as the current struck her. I studied all the instruments to make sure there were no mistakes possible. Nothing was wrong. Everything was exactly as it should be. Her lids fluttered, sank down, hiding her eyes. I moved from button to button on the many switches, taking her gorgeous body through the exact routine she had so carefully rehearsed me in. I must make no mistakes. I'd be better off perhaps if she were dead, but I would die without her. Mad though she drove me, I'd kill myself if I were denied the sight of her. I had worshipped too long, not from afar, but agonizingly close. I was careful.

She opened her eyes after fifteen minutes of the electrical routine, during which the whole laboratory crackled with unseen forces. And when I looked into those eyes I knew that a stranger —yet one amazingly like Greta Stard, sat in the seat of the many wires. In the eyes of this stranger, so straightly and unmistakably that their silent message made my heart leap into my throat and pulsate there, was recognition, and invitation. I thought that the contour of the face had altered slightly. The hair was even blacker. The brows had arched a bit more. Perhaps the shape of the body was a bit more voluptuous. Whatever the change, it was a different Greta Stard—but with Greta's body

that, for five years, I would have given my life to caress, and have my caresses returned.

I began the formula in which she had instructed me:

"Who are you?" I asked.

"I am Mariana Trayme, of course," she answered me, her voice soft and silken, and with a strange accent in it. It was a voice that purred, and suggested caresses. It was a voice that kissed the man who heard it, just as the eyes kissed him, just as the whole body strained toward him instinctively, as though it, in its entirety, would kiss him, too. I did not need to look at the family line of Greta Stard to know that Mariana Trayme was Greta Stard's great-great-great grandmother, who had died some hundred years before Greta's birth into this troubled world. She had, from the meager record, been a heartbreaker, and now I could believe it.

"Mariana Trayme," I whispered, "and you were born when?"

"In seventeen sixty-one, of course! How could you not know that? Or not know me?"

"And how old are you now?"

SHE cocked her head, coquettishly, and answered: "I am just twenty-two years old, Mr. Whoever-You-Are, as you would know if you knew the date, which is seventeen eighty-three! We *must* know each other, I take it— I can't imagine what's wrong with me that I can't seem to remember, for I've drunk but little—or I would not be sitting before you, undraped like this."

But she did not mind, in the least. I went on with the formula. My hands shook as I released her from the chair. My hands touched her flesh a time or two, quite by accident, and the electric current of her sped through me as the real current had just sped through the lovely body of Greta Stard. I had all but forgotten Greta Stard, in the presence of Mariana Trayme. But when I remembered that the body of Mariana was the body of Greta, madness took possession of me.

I don't know how I managed the questions Greta had told me to ask, but somehow I did. All they referred to were the facts in the life of whoever manifested herself in the body of Greta Stard. I simply put the "reincarnated" subject on the witness stand, and asked everything I could think of. It was Greta's real search for herself, in those who had lived before her, whose blood was in her veins. I hurried through it, my hands shaking, my body trembling with eagerness. And all the time the incomparable Mariana Trayme was half-smiling at me, drumming the chair-arms with delicate fingers, meeting my eyes with eyes that were so disturbing I still don't know how I managed my duty.

But it was done, finally, and I dropped my pen beside the pad.

Mariana Trayme said:

"I thought you'd never have done with your silly writing. I can't understand how any man can sit there like that, when I am sitting here like this, sir, and make marks on paper. Is it that at twenty-two I have already lost my allure for men? And you such a handsome, robust one, too!"

I rose to my feet, a bit unsteadily. I faced her. She rose to meet me. Her lips were trembling, a little moist. Her eyes were narrowed. Her little white teeth were visible, and *hungry!* I caught her in my arms, and all her body, as she stood on tiptoe to meet my lips, was a beating heart. For all of a minute we stood, kissing, entwined. Then I lifted her in my arms. Her arms were about my shoulders as I bore her into a shadowed corner, and her arms tightened, then relaxed, tightened and relaxed.

And when I sat with her upon the divan in the shadows, she murmured in my ears, words I had never expected to hear from the lips of Greta Stard, but which came all naturally from the lips of Mariana Trayme. They were words that one treasured, recalled in secret, yet never mentioned to a living soul, nor even spoke aloud when one was alone. They were words of endearment beyond endearment. . . .

How could I, I asked myself, take her back to that chair, and send her back and back into her own time, back into the grave, back to the dust whence she had come to me for a little while? How could I do that, when I had found perfection, as, she told me, she had? She—I did not tell her, but she perhaps sensed it—had crossed two centuries of time to find something she had never found in all her tempestuous lifetime.

But I had to take her back. Something deep within me sounded a warning that catastrophe would result if I did not. I could not imagine what catastrophe, but I knew that when I had a hunch of *that* kind, I had better heed it. In a way she sensed it, too, and clung to me when I put her in the chair, which she could not possibly have understood, as though she would never let me go.

I pressed the buttons, went through the regular routine.

In due time Greta Stard opened her eyes, stared into mine. I released her from the chair. She crossed quickly to the pad on which I had written, on which I had exactly recorded the time of the experiment. Then she looked at the clock on the wall, whirled to look again at me.

And the most abysmal hatred I had ever seen in the eyes of a human being looked out of Greta Stard's eyes, straight and deadly as daggers into mine!

CHAPTER II

VERBAL WHIPS

SHE said nothing about it, directly, but that one look of hatred told me that she *knew!* Physically, it meant less than nothing to her; mentally it meant a betrayal she would never forgive. Yet when she began reading the notes I had taken, she gasped, and seemed to forget it all. The name, Mariana Trayme, brought a gurgle of delight from her lips. And the sound of it made me remember, and wonder, with a dull sick feeling within me, just where the ashes of that long-dead lady might be lying at this moment—for Greta did not know for certain. Now Greta turned toward me. I did not note that she had clothed herself partially, until now. But when I noted I knew that never again would she be as indifferent to me as she had been. Thank heaven for at least that much, though it took her further away from me than ever.

"We've discussed this matter of heritage often enough, Trask," Greta Stard said, sitting down in the chair that must still be warm from the body of Mariana, "to have worked out some facts in the matter. Reincarnation is an old story, man's hunt for the truth. I hold that we have all lived before, many times. Maybe you and I, ages ago, even worked together on experiments like this, or at something similar. Maybe we were sweethearts once, unfortunately sweethearts, so that I do not desire you now. I inherit much from the males of my line, and the females. It is not inconceivable, then, that the countless 'mes,' back down the centuries in the past, have occasionally been men?"

"Not a doubt," I said, trying to forget that hatred I had seen in her eyes.

"I have often been a man, often been a woman. Those men, and those women, were *not* exactly I, for each of them had to live, and bear or beget children, before I could be I, as I am now. But if we adhere not too strictly to genealogical law, we must admit that . . . yes, you have often been a man, I have often been a woman, back down the generations."

"Then," said Greta, "let us continue with this experiment. I am not tired. The experiment has done nothing injurious to me. I want to gather all the data I can. After a time we will change, and you will make the trip into the past. Incidentally, I remember absolutely nothing that happened during the time you have set down on your record—not one thing. The last thing I remember is your eyes, fixed so intently upon me. Then they became just one eye, as the two drew together and merged. Then they were blotted out, until I saw you again. And Trask your face was deadly pale, and there was terror in your eyes—and guilt!"

I choked, and could say nothing. Greta went on:

"Since all my ancestors are in me, and the husband of Mariana Trayme was equally, with Mariana, my forebear, I would like . . ."

"I guessed what she would have said, and wondered why she broke short off without saying it. Again there was a warning bell, ringing deep within me. But I was, in effect, in thrall to this woman. No matter what she planned to do to me, I could no more leave her forever than I could fly to the moon.

"I can," she said, but after jumping much that she had first intended saying, I was sure, "become any ancestor I wish, if he or she were sufficiently like me."

A strange, but accurate, way to put it. I returned her to the chair. The routine began again. But this time she was clothed as for a journey, and I knew that never, barring accident, would I see Greta Stard as I had seen her during the last experiment. Again the subtle change. I studied her as it came about. Her shoulders broadened. Her face became coarse. Her hair changed, seemed to curl in upon itself, become coarser. Her chin and cheeks began to muddy, to change. . . .

Visibly and swiftly, more swiftly than I can set it down, Greta Stard was growing a luxuriant brown beard!

And then, her eyes opened! They were even more malevolent than the eyes of Greta Stard had been when she had looked at me and known the truth. They were a man's eyes. I was looking into the eyes of . . .

"I am Carter Trayme," said a deep masculine voice. "What is the meaning of this, anyhow? Am I a cuckold, that I am dressed as a woman?"

I looked at his clothing, Greta's clothing. His great bearish body had burst its seams. It was coming apart all over his body. Through the low neck of it, which burst asunder with a firecracker-like report, I could see a chest as hairy as that of an ape. My hands shook, as they had shook when I first looked into the eyes of Mariana, but for a far different reason. I did not think of danger to myself, for how could this man know anything about . . . about . . .

I released him, asked him to take the chair that Mariana had occupied before him. Then, I began to question him. He answered because he seemed unable not to. He got the words out utterly against his will, as though something far more powerful than his own great physique bade him answer me. But when I said I had got enough, his face was red with fury, almost purple, and his eyes were alight with rage.

"Who are you to question me like this? And how is it that you know of certain things that only I know, and Mariana? What place is this? Where am I? Who are you? Why this queer masquerade? Why are you garbed so strangely, like a man from another world?"

WELL he might ask that question, for to him the masculine garb of the twentieth century must have been strange indeed. He would have thought nothing of it, had I worn a powdered wig, and knee-breeches of silk. But how could I tell him anything? That I could not, or would not, only enraged him the more. He was ready to fling himself upon me. I was eager for just one thing; to get him back into that chair, send him crashing back to the ashes from which modern science had resurrected him. But I knew . . .

He suddenly shot out his hand, grabbed the pad on which I had been taking notes, from my hand. He almost choked with fury as he read what I had written—about his Mariana!

"So!" he said. "She has been here, to a rendezvous with you, a puling stranger? I had thought she had made an end of all that wildness she got from her own family, but it appears it isn't so! Well, I can't do anything to her. Unfortunately I love her too much to kill her. But at least I can make sure that it will never be *you* again!"

Then he lunged at me. There might have been something laughable, something hideously ludicrous, in this monstrous man, garbed in the burst-out clothing of Greta Stard, had it not been for the murder that looked out of his eyes. As he lunged at me, hands clawing at my throat, I thought: "Greta did this deliberately! She means for this man to kill me! But how, if he does, can she ever return to the laboratory? Has she thought of that?"

But of course she had, for while the blood of this man was in Greta Stard, and none of her blood was in him—because he had been dead a hundred years and more when she was born into the world—some of his mentality was hers, some of . . .

I was confused, could not figure it out. But this much I knew: If this man killed me, in some way that only a man could kill, Greta's will power could return this man to the chair after the killing, press the necessary buttons, and then emerge from the chair as Greta Shard, her vengeance on me for betrayal hideously complete. She could tell the police that a marauder had slain me. It was hellishly simple—and she had gone into this second stage of the experiment for the sole purpose of bringing it about.

I sidestepped, shot a left deeply into the pit of Carter Trayme's stomach. I shot a terrific right to his jaw. Both blows dismayed him, but did nothing to his courage. They hurt, too, but he was a big man. He knew nothing of this way of fighting. But he knew how to kick, and lashed out with his right foot. The toe—his feet had burst the shoes of Greta Stard asunder, but his feet were like iron—crashed against my jaw. I saw all the stars in the heavens as I went down, striking the back of my head on the floor.

Carter Trayme hurled himself at me, to come down on me with knees and feet and bludgeoning hands. I think both of us knew that we must use care in this battle, that we damage none of the scientific paraphernalia in the laboratory. I knew that if *I* did, this man would stay on here, and end in the electric chair in fact for slaying me. If I won the battle I could never send him back if the instruments were broken, for the real secrets of their construction were locked in the brain of Greta Stard.

And if Carter Trayme slew me, and the instruments were broken, what then? I could imagine what the mod-

ern world, outside this laboratory, would be like to him. And Greta Stard, as Greta Stard, would have vanished from the earth without trace.

So, I knew, and Carter Trayme guessed, or sensed—or was guided by the will of Greta Stard. And I got to my feet, fighting like a cornered coyote, fighting for my very life. Time after time I drove a left to his jaw, and a right, and a left. I felt his soft beard against my knuckles, time after time. I felt my knuckles bite into his flesh, to the bone. I forgot that somewhere within this creature whom I was reducing to a bleeding hulk, was the person, at least the spirit, of Greta Stard.

I went down, twice, and twice he got his fingers into my throat, and blood from the smashed nose, blood from his bleeding mouth, smeared upon my face. Twice I freed myself, and kept on fighting. After all, this man was an older man than I. He had been "picked up" before middle age, as nearly as I could tell, right at his fighting peak. I had not an old man to fight, and only the fact that I was even younger saved me from death.

I managed, after what seemed like an age of fighting for my very life, to down him with a right flush on the button. Even as I did so I had a surge of horror all through me. How could this be possible, that I was knocking out a man who had been dead a century and a half? I was actually fighting a corpse! I was also fighting Greta Stard! Just where, in the intricate maze of the generations, was the right answer? I couldn't even guess with any degree of accuracy, but the horror of the thought that I was trying to keep a man long dead from slaying me was a gruesome one to contemplate. But that did not keep me from breathing a sigh of relief when he went down heavily, and the breath went out of him in a great sigh.

I put myself to rights as best as I could, and as fast, for I didn't want him to come around and start on me all over again. I went over the laboratory, to find nothing amiss, none of the apparatus broken. That was the biggest relief of all.

I now caught Carter Trayme under the arms. It felt strange for my hands to touch the exploded garments of Greta Stard, but I fought off the feeling of unreality, and dragged the man to the chair of the experiment. I fastened him in, almost with a prayer. I pressed the various buttons. His eyes popped open a second afterward, and stared into mine with hatred that I knew would never die—that was probably even now stirring the ashes of the real Carter Trayme. He strained forward, but the chair had him, and I was safe.

"You meant for me to die, Greta," I whispered, as I watched the writhing, bloody body of Carter Trayme. "You tricked me, or tried to. But bear this in mind, my dear, I won't fall for any tricks—and above all, I'll never offer myself as a subject for your experiments! God knows, feeling as you must have, to bring this about, what you would do to me when I couldn't help myself!"

The body of Carter Trayme was shrinking swiftly. The shreds of Greta's clothing were hanging on it like ruptured pennants. The body of Greta Stard was returning to the world of to-day. Where she was when she was "away," I did not know, nor, if what she had said last time were true, did she. That was something she'd one day wish to know, of course.

The eyes of Greta Stard opened, finally, to look weakly, sicklily, into mine. I hurried to her, my heart in my throat and, surely, in my eyes. I released her, and she would have fallen on her face if I had not caught her. For

the dreadful beating I had given Carter Trayme had been given also to Greta Stard. Carter Trayme had been able to stand it; it had all but killed Greta Stard! She was a mass of cuts and bruises. Blood dyed her beautiful face, now deep sunken with fatigue. She was awfully, horribly close to death—a victim of a murderer, myself!

"Don't tell the police," she whispered. "Don't get a nosy doctor. I guess you'll have to do the best for me that you can! Take me into my room. Give me a drink. Bring me your notes!"

Her lovely body was in my arms, and very close against me—under the rags to which the bulging muscles of Carter Trayme had reduced her garments—as I entered her bedroom for the first time. My heart hammered with a weird excitement. For in her eyes I had seen no blame for me, for what I had done to her. I saw no hatred, no anger.

I saw only sickness, which I might cause to vanish with the care of a lover. I saw . . . I saw . . .

I saw many things that made me wonder, afterwards . . . after I . . . after she . . . after I had forgotten the first look of hatred, and took it for granted she had forgotten to hate.

CHAPTER III

Heart's Desire

PLAINLY Greta Stard was close to death from the brutal beating I had given her. If she died, I would rather die than live, and go mad. And she was in my care. Her lovely eyes—lovely in spite of the bruises around them,—looking into mine with a trust that I would never have believed them capable of showing, as I began to minister to her. First I removed those ripped and shredded clothing, and she did not mind. She only moaned when it was necessary to move her, and closed her eyes against pain that must really have been ghastly. Looking at her body, so delicate when compared to that of Carter Trayme, I wondered how she could live on. If, as Greta Stard, she had taken the blows I had handed out to Carter Trayme, her neck would have been broken a dozen times—every bone in her body would have been smashed asunder by my terrified fists. But the great body of Carter Trayme had protected her to some extent—and even so she was close to death.

I knew all her laboratory as I knew all the loveliness of Greta herself. I found the medicines, the unguents, the soothing oils. And while she lay upon the silken coverlets of her own bed, I applied them with fingers that trembled. I touched all her body with my hands, and tried to make those hands gentle. I loved her then as I had never loved her before, desire mixed with tenderness of which I would never have believed myself capable. For always, in mental pictures wherein I had possessed this woman, my urge had been to batter down, to hurt, to maim. Now I found my hands as gentle as those of a nurse.

And now and again I looked into her eyes, to find them very thoughtful as they met mine. There was gentleness in them, and dawning understanding of how it was with me. And it occurred to me, as it must have occurred to her, that since in beating the person of Carter Trayme, I had all but slain Greta Stard, in making love to Mariana Trayme I had also made love to Greta! I hadn't thought of it like that before, but that's how it must have been.

And here, under my hands, was the body, or a close semblance of it, which had carried me to heights of inexplicable ecstasy. But it was battered and broken and beaten, and must be cured of its hurts before . . . before . . .

Before what? As Greta regained her strength, and her loveliness and independence came back, would she not be again the Greta Stard who was without anything feminine except the form? I dreaded that possibility beyond all others, and yet if it came to pass so, what could I do to prevent it? With fear in my heart, as the days passed, and the nights, I looked into her eyes when I could, looking for the dawning of the old hatred—and not finding it. The gentleness seemed to increase instead, and something else—was it promise? Promise of all that for five ghastly years, I had hoped for? It was *still* too much to hope for.

At night, while she slept, and her beauty came back through the angry bruises my fists had made, I would go into the laboratory, to live over certain things, and to fight down the qualms I could not help entertaining. For during her waking moments Greta spoke often and often of what we would do together when she was well again. We had but scratched the surface of her experiments, she said, and when we had really delved deeply enough, we would find the answer, certainly and surely, to the scheme of creation.

I stood in the darkened laboratory, night after night when I could not sleep—certainly not in the distant room she had originally allotted me—and lived over the recent past. Time after time, in my mind, I lived through the ecstatic, unbelievable, inexpressible m o m e n t s fate had given me with Mariana Trayme. They would never come again, of course, save through the person of Greta Stard, and who could tell what the next few days would do to her? I felt Mariana, there in the laboratory with me.

And, time after time, I stood aside, a ghostly spectator, and watched myself in mortal combat with Carter Trayme. I saw the two shadow figures, there in the laboratory, fighting over an insult I had paid to Mariana Trayme. Carter Trayme had known his wife, and had tried to avenge her, only to be cast back into forgotten generations for his fury.

New dramas, beyond present conception, I knew, were to be lived and worked out in this laboratory, and I was afraid to face them. Frankly, when I knew this was true, I told Greta what I feared—though my fears were nebulous. Sometimes, when she called to me at night, and I went in and sat beside her, and held her hand, and stroked her body, I told her. Then I could not see her eyes, to know what thoughts they mirrored. Only her soft breathing told me that she was alive. Or sometimes her hands gripped mine convulsively, as though to reassure me.

BUT they never did reassure me, save for the briefest of intervals. If, I often thought, the thing I had most desired for so long, were to happen between us, then never again would I fear anything—for if I attained my heart's desire, nothing that could happen to me would be too great a price to pay. This, too, I told her, though not in just those words. I simply spoke in a way she could not mistake.

And there came a day when she walked into the laboratory with me, and stood beside me, holding my hand, and looked the place over. Her nostrils were quivering with excitement. She was eager to resume her labors. She looked at me when she sensed that I was watching her, and her eyes were still alight with that promise. Then, she faced me, and took both my hands in hers.

"Marvin," she said softly, "I have been a selfish girl, a terribly selfish girl. I have enjoyed being babied by you. If I hadn't come into the laboratory I might have gone on, allowing you to wait on me, and love me; but I have

come in, and the old call is too much. So, tomorrow we start again."

"You mean you have been well enough, for some time. . . ."

She laughed merrily, interrupting me. "I could have come back to work a week ago. But being babied was so delightful. And now, there is something else between us, something I know has been in your heart for years, but not in mine, to my dismay, now that I understand. I knew, when I came back, what had happened between you and Mariana. I knew for a certainty when your drubbing fists, upon the body of Carter Trayme, left their marks upon me. The thing I had hoped would never happen to me, at the hands of any man, actually happened. I knew, and joyed in it. I hated myself for the ecstasy. I hated you for having broken me down, even against my will. But the fact remains. . . ."

She turned her eyes up to mine again, looked deeply into mine. In her eyes was a caress I could not mistake. She moved a bit closer to me. She removed her hands from mine, ever so gently. She started to raise her arms, but never fast enough for me. I gathered her in my arms with all my strength. She moaned with the pain of my embrace, but she did not draw back. My lips went down to meet hers, eagerly lifted for my kisses.

I held her tightly for a long moment. Our bodies strained together with the age-old lure of the sexes. My hand went down the smooth curve of her back. Her nails bit into my shoulders.

Still with my lips pressed on hers, I lifted her in my arms, turned with her, carried her across her own threshold as though she had been a bride. But I never thought of her as my bride, as I knew she never thought of me as her husband. An heiress did not marry a bum! Not that, then, either of us thought of that.

Beside the bed where I had ministered to her hurts, I stood holding her, while moonlight came through the high window, and the sounds of New York City's streets came up to us like a lullaby.

"For days and nights," I murmured, my breath hot against her cheeks between kisses, "I have dressed and undressed you as though you were a baby. I have trembled when I did it. . . ."

"Have you forgotten how?" she answered softly. "Do your hands still tremble? I want what you want, my Marvin, to the ultimate ecstasy, the ultimate pain. And afterward. . . ."

"Afterward, what?" I asked.

"You will have no reason, surely, to fear anything—anything that may happen when we return to our work together."

And so, there in the moonlight, I saw her gorgeous body again, not as I had ever seen it, but as the lovely body of a woman who desired her mate with the most secret depth of her soul. I could even see her eyes in the moonlight, like two stars. Her lips were parted redly, murmuring. She murmured even those words Mariana had used, and which must have come down to her from Mariana herself. I knew for a certainty that she could never have used them before, to anyone, and no one would ever have passed them on, from mother to daughter to granddaughter.

Mariana had been perfection. Greta Stard was Mariana, and Mariana's daughters, and granddaughters, and all the wild free women of the Trayme and Stard families. She was everything a man could wish for, and much, much more. She was all delight, all ecstasy. And she held back nothing. What she felt she said. There were no inhibitions, nothing.

And when, however later it may have been—for I could never remember, though it may have been a night-long, or a minute—we were side by side and touching each other, as though neither of us wished to be separated again, she spoke softly, with a lilt of happiness in her voice:

"Now, are you afraid?"

"Of nothing in heaven or earth," I said. "Or beyond heaven, or under the earth. Whatever happens to me, this has paid for it in advance."

"And there is more," she replied. "More and always more. People like us, who delight in our delights, find that what happens is the greatest thing that can possibly happen, yet are amazed with each new experience, to and that ecstasy really has no end at all, but only grows. It promises to be unbearable, yet never is, really."

THREE days of experimenting passed, and three nights of joy that mounted beyond computation, and I was Greta's slave. Nothing she could do could possibly matter to me. I dreamed of her, even when we were working side by side. I remembered every little, slightest thing. I treasured every second of bliss, and looked forward to others to come.

"Tonight shall be the climax of delight," she told me, that third night. "It shall be payment in advance for tomorrow's experiment."

"And what, especially, happens tomorrow?" I asked.

"*You* will be the subject tomorrow, Marvin. I am curious about something. If we can be so much to each other, as we have been, then somewhere in the past, near or far, we have been something to each other before now. I am going to send you back to find the meeting place. We may have been our own ancestors, somewhere!"

I laughed with her, and forgot tomorrow in the glory of tonight. And that next day she was all business, as though she had forgotten the beauty and perfection of the night. Without fear I sat down, for the first time, in the chair whence Mariana had come, and Carter Trayme, and looked into the eyes of Greta, with all my love for her, I am sure, in mine, so that she could not miss it, and waited for her to touch the proper buttons.

She did. In the instant that the electrical current rendered me utterly powerless, my eyes were fast upon hers. And for the first time since she had come back to discover what had happened between Mariana and me, she allowed the truth to look out of her eyes. Oh, incomparable actress!

For the abysmal hatred exploding in her eyes shocked me into oblivion as surely as did the volts and the amperes her hands had sent crashing into my body.

I tumbled headlong into the past, carrying her hatred with me.

How long I was "away" I did not know. But gradually I came back. I focussed my eyes, which seemed strangely, horribly dim, on the face of Greta. There was mocking triumph in her face. I got down from the chair, wondering why I staggered. Something in her face sent me hobbling to the nearest mirror. It was a full-length mirror, and when I looked into it at first I could not prevent myself from whirling to see whether it were truly my own reflection there.

For an incredibly ugly old hag—who might have once have been a young, lovely *woman*—stared back at me from the cold, senseless surface.

I whirled on Greta. Her laughter, wild, savage, brutal, rang through the laboratory. I must have been mad, for I answered laughter with laughter—and mine was the senile cracked laughter of the ancient female hellion, the witch, the harridan. . . .

Then I discovered it wasn't laughter at all, but the weak sobbing of an old woman who has lived many decades too long. Greta walked to meet me, put her hands on her hips, and laughed in my face! I reached for her with hands that, I saw then, were like claws, or like the talons of a hideous bird of prey.

"To think," said Greta, "that I had to give myself to a bum, to a beast like Marvin Trask, to make vengeance complete! Yet even so, looking at you, I am convinced that it is worth it! For I have made up my mind to leave you exactly like this! I'll teach you, before I am done, what it means for a man like Trask to presume to possess a woman like me! If only I could rip out memory and cast it from me!"

"Let me come back, Greta!" I begged. "Let me come back! Help me into the chair. Press the right buttons. Let me come back as an old man, if you wish, but as a *man!*"

"You are as much a man, Grandma," she answered me, "as you will ever be again, no matter how often in my experiments you step into the chair and out again!"

CHAPTER IV

Black Horizon

AS the old hag, I had no shame whatever. I begged with all my might. I was a sight to behold as I demeaned myself. This old woman was some ancient grand dame of mine, no doubt about that, but she certainly gave me no pride of *my* ancestry. Just how a woman who must have been dead ages before either Greta or I had been born could know all I did of current events, I do not know. . . .

But then, all at once, I *did* know! I, as my own great-great—how many "greats" there might be—grandmere, became such grandmere through the body and person of Marvin Trask. Therefore, I was still Marvin Trask. I knew what was happening today, all right, but the instant I tried to do anything with the equipment in the laboratory I found my hands too gnarled and aged for any use whatever. I was an old crone. To make matters worse I was still dressed in the garments of Marvin Trask, which hung on me like a tent.

I was Marvin Trask, and the ancient one; so Greta Stard had been Mariana Trayme, without doubt. And as Mariana she had known very definitely all that had happened between Mariana and me. She had not needed to come back to find out. Then . . . then . . . she must herself, all those five years of my suffering with desire for her, have responded within her to the same desire. But, if she knew the history of Mariana, her flighty forbear, it was conceivable that she would fight down anything in herself that was like Mariana—and in so doing, perhaps, make a monster of herself.

That, I was sure, she had now done. For when I begged of her even on my bony knees, that she restore me to the form of Marvin Trask, no matter if she made him a very old man, empty of passion, she merely laughed at me. There were times, too, when she slapped me across the sunken cheeks. I could have hated her for such treatment of an old woman, but of course she knew that Marvin Trask was underneath the habiliments and the flesh of the old woman.

She never told me the old woman's name. She didn't need to. I knew it, naturally. Rina—"Granny" Rina, if you please—Gibbs. What a name, even for a harridan. And I found I knew a great deal about Rina—and wished I didn't, for she was a direct forbear of mine.

Naturally, I wished to be free of her.

Her life had ended on what we of today would call a very sour note indeed. She had been burned at the stake in Salem, for witchcraft. She was, I now knew, everything evil that had been charged against her. Just how such a one could produce children who had a right to live in a modern world, I couldn't for the life of me figure out, except that nature does her best to protect the seed of humanity, even against its own follies.

I was eager to have done with Granny Rina Gibbs, once and for all, but I never got anywhere with it, and I couldn't manage the paraphernalia myself, because Greta had carefully kept the essential routine secret from me. So, I began stalking her. I would find out just which buttons had to be pushed first. I would somehow manage to work the routine on myself. . . . No, that wouldn't do. The first shock sent the subject into a state of coma resembling hypnosis. I couldn't do it. I was utterly in the power of Greta Stard, who hated me with an obsession beyond anything I could conceive of. And I conceive of many strange and weird things, thanks to a progenitor like Granny Rina Gibbs, of whose body "Marvin Trask" was now a hellish caricature.

Greta, to make the story shorter— God knows I've no wish to drag out the unbelievable horror of it!—kept me as Granny Rina Gibbs for seven weeks. Not an hour passed, day or night, that I did not beg her for release from thralldom more hideous than ever these words can paint. I could not sleep. I would not permit her to sleep. I was wearing her down with my importuning; but at the same time I was building up her hatred for me—while I had all but forgotten how "Marvin Trask" had loved and worshipped Greta Stard.

"You old witch!" Greta said finally. "You're going to get your wish. I'm going to let you go back. I've even worked out the formula for it. Of course I always knew I'd do it, eventually. I can't stand your harping on it any longer. But if you think, when you are once more 'Marvin Trask,' that you will again be the lover of Greta Stard. . . ."

"I wish nothing of the sort!" I ranted at her, with the hardbitten, shrewish lips of Granny Rina Gibbs. "Put me back where I belong, and I'll never trouble you again, I swear it!"

But of course it did not occur to me that the passions of Granny Rina Gibbs, and those of "Marvin Trask," were widely at variance. They had to be. But even had I known, it was easy to promise.

"Back where you belong," said Greta Stard, thoughtfully. "Back where you belong. It's an idea, of course!"

Just what she meant, I had no way of knowing. All I knew was that I was soon to escape the odorous body of Granny Rina Gibbs, and it didn't matter what I got in her place. I would have preferred death, even—that part of me which was still Marvin Trask—though the body of Rina Gibbs clung to life with fearful tenacity. And I remembered the story of her burning, and hod she had cried curses out upon her destroyers in Salem, even when her legs had been burned off almost to her hips, and her hideous old body simply hung in gyves from the greenwood stake. Yes, she had been, and still was, plenty tenacious.

WE have agreed on a time when I shall sit in the chair again, and return as Marvin Trask, or, at least, as something definitely not Granny Rina Gibbs. That much Greta had promised me, and I believe her. She is just as tired of Granny as I am—and as the goodfolk of Salem became in Granny Rina's day.

I look at these words I have set down, in Granny Rina's hand, I suppose, for they certainly do not look like the writing of Marvin Trask, except so remotely that only a graphologist could see the resemblance, and shudder. There *is* something macabre in her handwriting. She may have been the witch they said she was, after all. I wondered where she had hidden her offspring away, when she was tried and executed, so that the executioners could not destroy the roots with the tree. She managed it somehow, that is all I know, else I myself would not be here.

This is the last, as Granny Rina, I shall write. I leave my pencil—my hand shakes so I can scarcely manage it, anyhow, both with age and excitement—and prepare to move to the chair. . . .

Very interesting, those notes of Granny Rina's. This is Greta Stard, writing her side of the story. I never in all my life hated a man as I hated and still hate, Marvin Trask. I hate him especially because of his grand, handsome body, which I have desired all these years. I know in my heart that I chose him from the grass at Central Park, not because his hands proved to me that he was a great scientist—I had recognized him from his pictures anyhow—but because of his body. I might as well say it, since nobody but myself will ever see these notes. I hate him because he made me realize my desire, how deep and abysmal it is, when I had sworn never to become the mistress of any man. And when Mariana Trayme stepped down from the chair . . . well, she had no inhibitions, and there was just enough of her in me, before that, to make me step over the line. And Marvin Trask, who loved me, and should have protected me, even from myself, did nothing of the sort.

That the ecstasy he mentions was shared by me has nothing to do with it.

He should have protected me from knowledge of such ecstasy, for it has no place in the life of a great woman scientist. I am determined now that it shall be destroyed.

Granny Rina Gibbs has gone under the first spell of my marvelous instruments for searching the subconscious and bringing it forth. My machinery is more efficacious than even the dreams of the would-be time-travelers. How can love and desire be allowed to stand between a scientist and those vast and mighty things of which she would be capable if she could but forget her femininity?

An interesting change is taking place in Granny Rina Gibbs just now. I am sending her back further into Marvin Trask's ancestry than I have ever sent anybody, or allowed myself to be sent. She went back with no conscious desire for anything, except to be free of Granny Rina Gibbs, so there is no telling *what* may happen. However, her body is getting bigger through the middle, becoming squatty. Her forehead. . . .

Great God! What have I done to Marvin Trask! What have I done to myself? God . . . God. . . .

Excerpt from a story that appeared next day in all New York City newspapers:

"It was something surpassing the imagination of Edgar Allan Poe's 'Murders in The Rue Morgue.' The policeman who invaded the laboratory of Doctor Greta Trask could not believe their eyes. Many things about it all must remain inexplicable, since obviously the manuscript left behind by the laboratory worker, or workers, depending on whether one can believe any part of their 'notes,' must be the work of a madman, or even two madmen.

But this is what the police found: A giant anthropoid ape, bigger than any ever brought to this hemisphere, gone berserk in the Stard laboratory. The ape—a giant female—had caught up Greta Stard in its monstrous arms, and was slowly pulling her apart, as a moron pulls apart a fly plucked from a windowpane. At first the officers were afraid to fire on the ape, lest they slay Greta Stard. But then they knew that Doctor Stard was already dead. After all, she had to be. Her head was missing from her shoulders. They found it later in the chair which Greta Stard used in her experiments.

"The police, when they realized this, opened fire on the ape. They heard their bullets, fully a dozen of them, crash into its hideous body. The ape roared at them—and a change came over the creature. It squatted on its haunches, with blood streaming down its chest, and cradled what was left of Greta Stard in its great arms. Some of the officers say that it crooned at the bloody corpse, that it even tried to kiss it. This, of course, is absurd. What could apes know of kissing?

"Do apes have tear ducts? That is a question others will have to answer eventually. In any case, certain of the officers insisted that the ape actually wept over the dismembered body of Greta Stard.

"Just what the notes stated, about which the officers of the law were so mysterious, will perhaps never be known. The police have decided to make the notes a part of the queer record in the case, but to keep them from the press. Perhaps it is just as well, for that there was something strange, almost *other*, about the affair, seems certain. For the most careful investigation has failed to produce information as to whence the ape could possibly have come!"

The End.

PERFECTIONIST
BY JOHN WALLACE
Author of "Hell's Hallowed Housewives," etc.

And then she was in the arms of the ugliest of the sub-men

THE tall man's face was of a waxy hue which seemed almost transparent; his cheek bones were sunken, cadaverous, his hands long and bony.

He moved across the glittering chromium laboratory, the walls of which were sombre in black velvet. Slowly, with a strange gleam in his deep-set black eyes, he removed the shirt from his gaunt unpleasant frame. The shirt was the sheerest silk and its source was a common weed of rural meadows—for now, in the year 2002, the things which had been regaded as minor miracles in the year 1939, were commonplace.

"My girdle, Maria," the gaunt man said, cackling mirthlessly.

A thin ugly woman, who greatly resembled the men in general appearance, turned from the laboratory table. Her dark eyes were expressionless slits. In her hands was a girdle, a garment of metallic cloth. She fitted it around the man's bony unhandsome body; it extended from his waist up under his arm-

PERDITION

pits, fit snugly, comfortably.

"It is perfect," the woman said in a hollow sombre tone. "That is well. We have completed our research in time, Malson—in time, in time!"

The maze of tubes, machines, filters, and instruments were like bizarre inanimate ghosts as the last rays of the setting sun filtered through the great circle of glass in the west side of the laboratory.

"The sun—great source of life and beauty and love!" the gaunt man cackled.

"The sun! The sun!" There was a faint smile, bitter and vengeful, upon the woman's face as she echoed the man's words hollowly.

For long moments they gazed through the circle of glass at the great ball of fire setting beyond the western horizon; gazed not so much in adoration as in triumph, for now—

"Its secret is ours, our slave!" the gaunt man muttered, gazing, eyes glit-

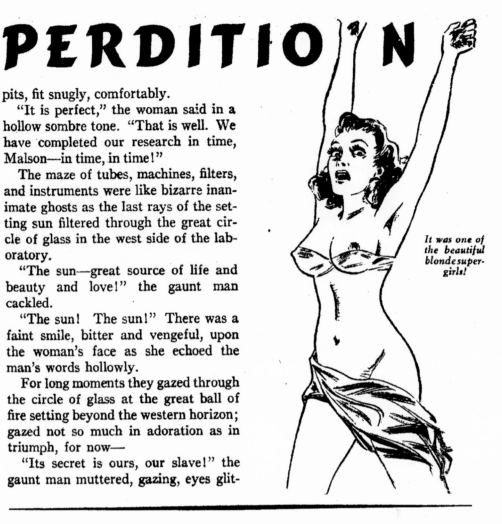

It was one of the beautiful blonde super-girls!

This was the year 2002, and you didn't rejoice when a beautiful girl said she'd be your bride!

---

tering.

Slowly he picked up the flat maze of black tubes and peculiar black box with its rows of nozzles and its four black buttons which were the controls. . . .

Far across, on the north side of the streamlined city, the great auditorium of the Society For Natural Selection was packed. The auditorium was spotlessly white within, ideally ventilated, of ideal temperature. For it was symbolic of the aims and methods of the Society.

Before the center microphone of the great stage, a bronzed young man stood alone. On one side of him were the complicated television machines which would broadcast the sights and sounds of this meeting to all America. And on the other side of him, to his right, were a dozen small box-like booths in which sat things which were, technically, humans.

The young man was well over six feet tall, perfectly formed, handsome, his skin glowing with vitality and robust health. He spoke and his voice was rich, vibrant:

MADE ROMANCE IN THE TWENTY-FIRST CENTURY A.D.!

"My friends, this is a most momentous occasion in American history, in the history of the world. It is the beginning of a new era, an era of which the more enlightened have been dreaming for a century, but which has been deterred by the musty laws and theories of yesteryears.

"As you know, we have revised the conception of the theory of natural selection. Nature, the mating instinct within us all, is not to be trusted. Its fallacies are multifold, its tendencies through history have been to propagate the unfit with the result that the fittest have tended gradually to have their superior characteristics dragged down to levels far beneath them. Mediocrity, in heredity is ever dominant. In the mating of a superior being with a mediocre, the odds are roughly nine to one that the offspring will be mediocre. The inevitable end-result of this haphazard and unscientific mating will be, necessarily, a deadly bogwallow of mediocrity. The percentage of genius has fallen steadily, alarmingly, in the past century. All progress since medieval times has resulted from the superior capabilities of a tiny proportion of mankind. Except for the work of these few superior beings, mankind would even now be dwelling in caves, crudely hunting food with a club, wearing loin cloths ineptly fashioned from the skins of dead animals . . ."

IN the front row of the great balcony, Jere Jamieson, ace reporter for the monthly Scientific Journal, rapidly jotted his impressions of this great gathering and all that went on. To Jere Jamieson, this was the most portentous scene he had covered in years. Portentous not only in the fact that the findings and recommendations of this society might reshape the application of eugenics, but also in the fact that Jere Jamieson's fiancee was one of the chosen ones, one of the nearly perfect ones who occupied the seats in the first floor of the auditorium now. These balconies were reserved for the unselected hoi-polloi, so to speak—the ordinary humans who had been fortunate enough to procure seats.

Jere Jamieson could see her down there now—a golden girl of perfect health and physical beauty: his Shirley, whom chance had caused to pass his way, to make them find mutual love. Love which was forbidden her by the rules of the Society.

"As you also know," the bronzed and perfect young man continued into the microphone, "this great state was fortunate enough to have for its governor some thirty years ago a man who was a scientist, a eugenicist, a man willing to risk wide censure that mankind might ultimately be saved, improved, brought, indeed, near to perfection. He set apart the northern section of this city, virtually isolated it, that his theories might be visually substantiated. He selected several hundred humans of the highest type—both physically and mentally— kept them isolated in this community of the superior. The result—you who sit before me in the ground-floor section of this auditorium, you who are the obviously superior offspring of obviously superior parents—*you* are the result, the living proof that if mankind is to find salvation, to ascend hereafter instead of descending steadily as heretofore, *only the truly superior in both mind and body must be permitted to propagate!*"

There was a moment of silence, followed by a low buzzing undercurrent of sound tinged with anger from the common people in the balconies.

The bronzed and perfect young man held up an adjuring hand and smiled an understanding smile. "I anticipate the reaction of resentment from you and your reason for it. You do not understand fully the plan as we have outlined it and as the present governor of this state and the President of these United States himself have understood and approved it. In brief the plan is this: all save a fraction of the top quality of our citizens shall be sterilized—"

Another buzz of resentment greeted this statement.

The young man held his hand up again, calmly continued: "—That is, perhaps only two percent shall be permitted to propagate: those two persons, male and female, who are the finest mentally and physically, of any given group of one hundred persons. But you who are of the remaining ninety-eight have no reason to be alarmed or to resent this. As human beings hoping for the betterment of the race, you should rejoice and exult. For *you* shall suffer in no way, and posterity shall benefit immeasurably. Know this: the act of sterilization, as now performed, shall deprive you of *none* of the pleasurable and natural emotional functions of love and marriage. It shall deprive you *only* of the capacity for gestation, for propagating your steadily deteriorating selves. True, the population total will drop sharply in the second generation beyond those of you who are now adult—the *quantity* shall be very small, but the *quality* shall be amazingly higher in average. Within the course of the next two centuries the population shall have risen to virtually its present quantity again and, vitally important, the *average* man will be as fine a specimen as the best of us who stand here now upon display as proof of the soundness of our beliefs."

As an individual of inferior physique who loved a girl of patently superior body and, perhaps, mind, Jere Jamieson felt a surge of resentment within him. But as a good reporter, he viewed and listened with impersonality. He wrote

rapidly, listened to the buzz around him, studied faces. Strangely enough, the only two faces in the horde of common people around him which seemed undisturbed and unresentful were the faces of the two homeliest in the balcony: a gaunt cadaverous man and woman, each dressed in black, and each with smiles, enigmatic, upon their unattractive faces. They sat several seats away from Jere, in the front row of this first balcony.

"Know too," the obviously superior young man continued, "That our organization functions in every land, and the rulers of every nation are upon the point of agreeing to our plan if America will lead the way as evidence of its sincere belief. Our belief is that the only real natural selection is the natural selection of science and wisdom—for wisdom is greater than any single thing in nature as you define the word. To *prove* our contentions, you who are here in the auditorium and you millions who watch and listen through the medium of television—*I shall pick at random individuals from our selected group, to give them mental, spiritual and moral tests and to display the perfection of their physical selves to you.* If you please, the spotlights!"

FROM the deep face of the balcony below Jere Jamieson's feet, two light orange spotlights shone down into the audience of superior humans on the first floor. The spotlights focused upon eight people at random—four young men, four young women. They arose, walked up the stairs onto the stage.

The young man who was chairman spoke again, pointing to the twelve misshapen and stupid-appearing humans who sat in the booths on the stage at his right: "Here you observe the offspring of various combinations: brilliant father and mediocre mother, brilliant mother and stupid father, or two commonplace parents. These offspring, you will observe, have many things in common: unshapely, unhealthy bodies, inferior brains, inferior moral sense; inferior competence in every respect. And the percentage of such as these has become alarmingly high, is increasing. Eventually their kind will be dominant everywhere, will constitute mankind in total. I ask four of them to come here, that you may contrast the product of haphazard nature with the product of selective science."

The nearly perfect eight stood there gracefully in the orange spotlights, their bodies beautiful in the filmy clothes they wore and the light of high intelligence shining from their faces. The four inferiors, selected at random by the spokesman's assistant, came out of their booths stupidly, walked forward in a shambling gait.

And then a strange thing happened. The sort of thing Jere Jamieson least expected.

The four perfect and extremely beautiful girls began to act most peculiarly. Their shapely breasts rose and fell as they breathed more deeply than was normal, their mouths parted and their lips, of warm beauty, trembled sensuously. Their hips and torsos, intriguingly concealed beneath the filmy white dresses and mesh lingerie which they wore, quivered erotically, writhed slowly, though none the less suddenly, as in some pagan mating dance.

The spokesman, his attention focused momentarily upon the four degraded men, was saying into the microphone:

"You will observe the dull phlegmatic bestiality of the countenances. Such men as these, if allowed to continue propagating will become the standard of normalcy. These eight, on the other hand, though only the first generation of scientific selection, are close to perfec—"

He broke as, from the corner of an eye, he observed one of the girls approaching one of the ugly brute-like men. In her eyes there was a gleam of spellbound fascination, of incredible desire.

"To me," she murmured, "to me you are handsome in your ugliness. You—you are the mate for me. I shall raise your standards of being to my own. My life is meaningless without love. All women desire love, and love is forbidden us who are of the Society. We may not love until we have achieved the mental and physical heights of our development. I cannot wait. I choose, as ordinary women may choose—*for no reason readily apparent to others!*"

The girl, a lovely brunette, trembled. Her perfectly developed bosom rose and fell in fiery gusts of passion as, with a violent gesture of desire, her hands swept up to her white lace bodice, ripped it downward. The beautifully molded white mounds of her young breasts appeared, their charm sufficient to drive any normal man into a frenzy of elemental action.

Almost savagely, she ripped the dress and the mesh lingerie from her body. For a moment she stood there thus, as lovely and appealing as the ultimate dream of the most ardent erotic perfectionist. A trembling, vibrant thing of warmth, of love's essence. Then she flung herself wildly toward the malformed man who was so greatly her inferior. Flung herself at him with low cries of rapture, primitive passion in very movement of her delectable body.

The result was unexpected.

For the malformed man, who might logically have been expected to meet her with an inflamed avidity equal to her own, suddenly snarled deep in his throat, grasped one of the girl's arms, twisted it brutally behind her, placed a foot in the middle of her back and forced her to the floor of the stage.

"I hate you!" he exclaimed in a hoarse guttural voice. "We all hate you! We'll tear you apart, so you won't ever put us up here to gloat over no more, paradin' your brains an' bodies in front of us like peacocks an' makin' us feel the scum of the earth! We don't mate with the likes of you! Tear 'em apart, men!"

HE gestured to the three beside him on the stage, and to the eight others who sat in the booths. The intense quick savagery of his crude uncultured voice aroused them more quickly than anything else he might have done, as animals in the jungle become suddenly murderous, vicious, at the sound of savagery from another of their own kind.

The eleven other unfortunate inferiors plunged toward the girls and the young men who were so near to perfection. Plunged swiftly, clumsily, but with a power, a mob fury, which gave them strength beyond themselves.

The spokesman and the other four young men who were near-acmes had been staring in astonishment, frozen where they stood by the unexpected turn of events—the same as all the people in the vast audience were petrified.

But the shock was only temporary. As two of the sub-men grasped the nude super-girl, placing their feet against her stomach and twisting mightily at her arms in the endeavor to tear those arms from their sockets, the super-men plunged into action. But they were outnumbered twelve to five and, though they were much better physical specimens than the sub-men, the latter fought with the berserk fury of men who have long nursed a grievance which has burned deep into their souls in the fires of hate.

One of the sub-men produced a knife from his pocket, slashed the bodice from a beautiful blonde super-girl and lashed at her body. Another of the sub-men dived at her, carried her to the floor in a crushing flying tackle. He placed his knee on her throat, held her down, as the man with the knife pounced. The latter slashed at the girl's breasts, ripped through them savagely. The girl twisted, screamed horribly from the pain as blood spurted, bathing her healthy white skin in twin geysers of red.

Another of the sub-men jerked from his pocket a sharply jagged instrument which resembled a currycomb, bestially raked the lacy skirt from a redheaded super-girl, knocked her to the floor and raked his instrument of torture down the glowing skin of the delicately lovely thighs; raked deep, making incoherent animal sounds at the sight of her warm blood seeping from the deep rivulets. It was as the sight of some small and sharp-toothed creature of the jungle lusting for the sweet strength of some helpless prey.

The sub-men, not powerful enough to pull the arms from the first girl's sockets, twisted her arms behind her until each arm snapped terribly with a sound like the breaking of a stick of kindling wood. When her arms were limp, as she lay there moaning in agony, they descended to her legs. Each grasped a leg, braced his feet and they pulled together in opposite directions in an attempt to break the sockets, to split the girl's body up the middle as they might split the trunk of a tree.

Having hideously mutilated the blonde girl's breasts, the sub-man with the knife lashed downward, split her stomach deeply. That done, he sprang to his feet and lunged for the remaining girl, a brunette who was thus far untouched, for the reason that she was in the hot embrace of one of the young super-men, kissing him intensely, trembling in his eager arms as he fumbled at her with a possessive avidity.

Pandemonium reigned, on the stage and now in the audience. After its first few moments of shocked amazement, the audience found its voice. From the balconies, the common people cried:

"Perfect in morals, are they?"

"Super-men! Why don't they protect womanhood?"

"They're as bestial as the sub-men! Fraud! Delusion!"

Jere Jamieson, sitting forward in his seat immediately over one of those orange spotlights, was frozen for a moment in incredulity and then—his thoughts took the personal trend. He thought of Shirley, Shirley the golden super-girl down there in that audience of super-humans. Shirley, the girl he loved and who loved him devotedly in turn—loved him, though Jere Jamieson was scrawny, anemic, unhandsome physically in nearly all respects though his brain was nearly as acute as that of any young super-man there below.

His brain reeled momentarily at the spectacle on that stage. His brain seemed to hum in his own ears, like the sinister undertone of a rattlesnake.

Though the unexpected scene of erotic terror had been proceeding for but a few brief seconds, Jere had observed, was observing now, several things which astonished him even more: three of the five super-men were actually competing now with the sub-men for the savage pleasure of mutilating and torturing the girls! Two of them tore the sub-man away from the red-headed girl, tore his rake-weapon from his hand and began to rake her body and breasts. The third leaped for the brunette, sank his teeth into her throat in the manner of a hungry beast, bore her to the floor.

THE other two, one of them the superb spokesman, fought heroically. But they were badly outnumbered and had no weapons, whereas the sub-men, berserk, had doubled their strength.

What was the cause of this mad phantasmagoria? Jere Jamieson asked himself this question frantically as he stared. That low rattlesnake buzz was still in his ears, persistent, unceasing, sinister. It seemed so real—and yet . . . Had he gone mad?

No. It was all real. Now, the super-men and a few of the super-girls were surging toward the stage, leaping up the steps on each side of the stage, to stop the melee.

But as they approached it, as the vanguard came into the beams of the great orange spotlights, an amazing thing happened! The super-men suddenly stiffened, clutched at their bodies and then, like some fantastic nightmare, their legs and arms and bodies began to shrivel!

To *shrivel*, to *shrink* so that their limbs and bodies began to resemble those of hundred-year-old men! Slowly they sank to the floor, gasping, their tongues swelling out of their mouths hideously.

"Shirley! Don't go up there!" Jere screamed piercingly, as he saw the girl he loved starting up the steps to the right.

Pandemonium! Bedlam! Incredible horror! Then Jere's mind, so unusually sharp for a common man in this twenty-first century, made a wild deduction: those spotlights! The first madness of eroticism and now this horror—all had occurred in those beams!

Jere looked about him searchingly, terror and panic sharpening his senses. The common people about him were standing up, shouting like animals, quite senseless in their fear and excitement after the fashion of emotional mobs since the beginning of time.

Screaming, yelling, shouting in a frenzy. Frenzied all.

No. Not all!

Not those two gaunt ugly people in black who were several seats to Jere's right, next to the rail, directly above the center of the one great orange spotlight! Not those two. They sat there calmly, their faces hard, immobile. And as Jere stared his eyes and ears found clues almost simultaneously:

That low buzzing sound like a rattlesnake! It seemed to emanate directly from the gaunt man's body! Jere listened intently, and as he listened he looked. Looked at the man and woman, looked in front of them, into the orange spotlight which came from the balcony face beneath them.

Yes! In that light orange beam of the spotlight were two narrow foreign rays—one a dark orange, the other almost a blood red. Both man and woman were sitting forward against the balcony rail, so that their bodies were almost touching the legitimate big orange spotlight beam.

Jere hesitated a moment. He realized that it might mean sudden horrible death to him—and yet . . .

Grimly, he arose, stepped back into the tier of seats above him, shoved several of the mob down into their seats, crept to a position behind the gaunt man. Then—

Jere reached forward, grasped the man's arms, pinioned them behind the great gaunt frame. The man whirled with an evil snarl, arose.

Jere Jamieson didn't hesitate. He pulled back his right fist, threw it with all the power in his scrawny, wiry body. It thudded solidly against the man's jaw, caught him off-balance. The man toppled backwards, the rail caught his knees from the rear and, with a ghastly, fearful scream he toppled over into the surging mass of super-humans thirty feet below.

The gaunt woman turned on Jere viciously, her sunken eyes monstrous with hate and fury. "Scum! Fool!"

she hissed, as the blood-red ray, sharp and murderous, flashed out from beneath her breasts.

Jere felt a terrible searing pain in his left arm and shoulder. The world about him seemed hideous, grotesque, as with one last despairing effort he smashed his right fist to the gaunt woman's jaw. Then Jere pitched forward on his face, hearing the screams and shouts around him, the fury of a mob gone berserk. . . .

He awakened, and the room was spotless white, with the immaculateness of the modern infirmary, and he saw a lovely golden girl kneeling beside his bed crying softly.

"Shirley!" Jere exclaimed.

SHE lifted her lovely face, with the warm intelligent eyes, against his face and sobbed: "Oh, Jere, darling! Thank God it was only your arm she hit with that dreadful atrophine ray! You saved the lives of dozens, perhaps hundreds of us. Oh, Jere! No. No! Don't feel for your arm!"

But Jere had already felt, felt a shriveled nerveless rope-like thing that could no longer be called an arm. He took a deep breath and asked quietly: "Who were they, darling? And why, why—"

"Their names are—are Maria and Malson Pendexter," Shirley murmured, sobbing a little between words. "They were overpowered, tortured into telling their story several hours ago. They both have brilliant scientific minds but they are anti-social, embittered against mankind, for two reasons: as you know, the atrophine ray has been the perfect cure for cancer, in use some four years now. Its discovery was credited to another scientist, mysteriously dead these past three years. Malson Pendexter murdered him—because the man stole the secret of the atrophine ray from Pendexter, deprived him of the credit, the gain, the fame which was his due.

Naturally he was embittered. For years he had been working on the theory that there is a sub-ray of the sun which stimulates and strengthens erotic desires. The basis for his belief is the exceptional virility and passion of peoples living near the equator, where the sun's rays are strongest.

"His theory proved correct. By dint of his genius and much hard effort, he isolated that sub-ray, learned how to concentrate it, to store it, to propel it on electricity. He used it and a powerfully concentrated atrophine ray—his sister Maria handled that atrophine ray, as you know too well—on us tonight, propelling them along the spotlight to keep them concealed as much as possible. He and his sister hated us doubly—we are nearly perfect, they are ugly, have been denied all normal emotion and love life; and too, our theories would improve the human race, which they hated. And the horrible part is: nearly all that dreadful scene was televised to millions. It may take us years to regain popular confidence after our degradation in the eyes of millions."

"It will take you not years, but *centuries*," Jere murmured, sighing. "It would have anyway. From the beginning of time, man in the mass has been opposed to any change, has been suspicious of it, has hated it. Man in the mass has always fought for his selfish, petty rights—never for the betterment of mankind as a whole. His puerile ego will not permit it. His basic emotions cannot be changed. You are proving that right now. By the logic of your Society it is impossible for you, a perfect woman, to love me, a very unhandsome, unattractive man. Yet you do. You want children by me, and I by you. The right to select one's own mate, to propagate, is imbedded in us so deeply, so fiercely, that we, and millions like us, would fight to the death to preserve that right—no matter how the good of mankind in general may suffer."

Shirley lay her cheek upon his and sobbed half in happiness, half in bitterness, torn between her two loves.

"Alas, my dear, mankind will probably go on in much the same old way to the mythical millennium," Jere murmured, sighing. "Fumbling, bungling, suffering, living and dying haphazardly, touched only by the futile everyday comforts of scientific product—never by the essentials, the deep essentials, of wisdom and knowledge. You see, my dear, the aims and beliefs of your Society have something unconquerably against them: those aims and beliefs are much too sensible ever to be accepted by mankind in the mass. . . ."

GIRLS FOR SATAN'S UTOPIA
BY BRENT NORTH
Author of "Horror in Hollywood," etc.

Girls!—Beware the man who is at once sub-ordinary lover and extraordinary scientist!

INSIDE the spotlessly hygienic thankorium of Doctor James Bass, of Zenith City, U. S. A., four young couples stood before the rostrum, to be joined in wedlock simultaneously. Healthy young people, yet somewhat blase and languid. All need for haste, for strain, for bustle and confusion, had long since vanished from the civilized sections of earth. Nature and the elements were harnessed slaves of man.

Kirth Jonas, historian, sat in one of the front rows of the thankorium and smiled wryly. And as he thought about it all, the wryness changed first to bitterness and then to downright anger. There was an irritating ache in his head. Until tonight he had regarded marriage tolerantly, as the last of the quaint and sentimental holdovers from antiquated centuries.

This was the year 2939, and professional historians such as Kirth Jonas frequently delved into the archives to read ancient volumes, to play phonograph records or to run yellowed motion picture films which detailed the manners, customs and ways of life practiced in the primitive dark ages of the Twentieth Century. That era seemed elemental now. For life had changed in externals. Modernity was one of the few words which never became dated; it stood always for the history of progress to date.

All things but one had changed.

There was a maximum of economic and scientific efficiency. Super-utilities, processes and all manner of inventions about which men had never so much as dreamed in the year 1900—these things were now as commonplace as bicycles had been one thousand years before. They were accepted as commonplace for the reason that the changes had been so gradual that man had taken them for granted, as had been man's habit since the beginning of time. Life was a scientific Utopia in all respects but one. . . .

The angry ache persisted in Kirth Jonas' head. He glared at the connubial couples before the rostrum. What archaic nonsense! Sentimentality! Kirth Jonas could see the same aversion in the faces around him. In all the faces. The absurdity of this archaic custom seemed to impress them all, suddenly.

For mating was founded now upon a sounder basis than had been the case centuries before. It was recognized now that the mating instinct was universal and hence fallible. A mere written agreement, terminable at the will of either party, was all that was now necessary and *this* long ritual was mere flambuoyant kneeling to an outmoded tradition.

Actually, this thankorium made no pretense of being religious. Only the outer form remained. The deities now accolated were not mysterious and infinite beings made in the image of man, but symbols of a practical scientific construction. For it was now generally believed that Science held the key to all things, animate and inanimate.

Kirth Jonas' head ached too greatly for him to rationalize his irritable sudden aversion. All except the impassive middle-aged Beacon Terwillig, who stood on the far side of the pulpit, were glaring, muttering. The Beacon stood there with an expression of dull reverential interest upon his rotund face.

As Doctor James Bass intoned the long marriage ceremony, Kirth Jonas thought irately: "Three days from now I, *too*, go through that archaic and meaningless rigmarole just to please the girl I love, as the ancient phrase goes. That's my reward for choosing a choirus singer for my mate." Marella, the girl Jonas was to wed, sang in the choirus of this thankorium as did these four girls now being married to their swains.

(The coined terms such as thankorium, beacon and choirus were semi-satirical play on words in common usage several centuries previously, and appropriate to the new form of accolade).

The doctor himself was glaring now, incredibly enough. Glaring over his spectacles at the four young couples. "—and do you vain young fools," he snarled, "take each other through this needless vanity of ceremony to be the stupidly lawfully wedded mates of each other? Do you, Bette Barton, take Edward Ennis to be—"

The girl, Bette, had been glaring at her husband-to-be for some seconds past. At the doctor's words, she suddenly blurted:

"No! The swine has big ears and talks through his nose!"

She reached out suddenly and slapped her groom-to-be hard upon his face. His face contorted in rage and he slapped her in return.

This acted as a sort of spark, which ignited a conflagration of furious confusion. The incipient brides and grooms clashed in a melee that for sheer wildness had not been exceeded for many years in Zenith City. At the start it was mere savage ire and irritation. Such a scene would have been considered sacrilege in the Twentieth Century, but not here—for the deity reverenced was an intricate scientific symbol which reposed in a grotto back of the rostrum.

Bedlam reigned.

Kirth Jonas breathed heavily, felt a sudden urge to maim, to mutilate. Women now, as in centuries past, were the natural enemies of men—using their allure to lead men to spiritual and financial ruin! He had never felt this consciously before, but he felt it now with a recklessness which caused him no amazement.

One of the near-grooms jerked a small silvery instrument from his pocket, pressed a button and—before the eyes of onlookers, the girl's white dress, of an artificial silk much more fragile and alluring than the kind spun by worms centuries ago, slowly turned brown and dropped from her delectable young body in the form of a powdery dust.

"The disseminator!" another young man cried. "Close the focus! Make holes in—"

The silvery instrument had thrown a soft purple ray over the girl's body, and was snapped off as her clothing fell away. Now it came on again, a single pencil-like purple beam.

It bore viciously at the girl's lovely white body and, slowly, slowly, a small round aperture appeared in her hip. Little brownish bits of dust fell from her, much as sawdust falls from the boring of a knothole. The girl screamed shrilly, shuddered. But she did not fall —merely stood there stiffly, staring with horror-laden eyes.

Kirth Jonas sprang to his feet, as did the others in the assemblage, intent on interfering, aiding in the torture, or getting closer for a better view. But they were halted suddenly.

Another young man whirled on the guests, a larger silver instrument in his hand and a murderous look in his pale blue eyes.

"Don't interfere! Stay where you are, or I'll have you turning into dust before you can take two steps!"

He meant it. They knew it. They crouched there, tense, but afraid. They stared.

"I've heard of that ray!" someone shouted. "It's a closely guarded government secret! How—what right have *you*—"

"Maybe we work for the government," the man with the bigger instrument sneered. "Maybe we had access to the secret. If you think we haven't, move closer!"

Nobody moved closer.

The other would-be brides and grooms ceased fighting abruptly, stared in frozen disbelief. The young man with the pencil disseminator ray had a cruel gleam in his eyes, as the nude girl who was to have been his bride leaned stiffly back against the rostrum. Two of the brown holes were completely through her body now, and a third was being bored above them to complete a sort of triangle.

"The nice part of this ray is that it cauterizes as it goes," the young man gloated. "It doesn't kill unless it bores through one of the major vital organs. Merely makes the holes. I like the triangle design. Since Eve, women have been fond of triangles. Each one of these four almost-brides shall have a triangle—through and through!" He chortled at his grim jest.

"Don't be hoggish, Lorin!" one of the other grooms shouted, his mouth twisted sadistically. "This female whom I was about to marry is an unconscionable shrew. Let me teach her. Remember you owe me—"

The young mman with the pencil-ray finished boring the third hole, and the girl no longer screamed. She merely leaned back, stiff with terror, her brown eyes open in a frozen stare. Her almost-husband glared at her sardonically, passed the silver instrument to his friend.

The latter seized it eagerly, hit his bride a terrific clout which knocked her back against the platform, and put the ray at a half diffusion focus. The girl's filmy upper garments turned to dust, sifted to the floor.

She was a luscious brunette, with beautiful white breasts. As she breathed deeply in her frantic terror, her breasts tossed sensuously, inflaming her lover to heights of torture-lust. Grasping her by the hair, he twisted her head back cruelly, focused the pencil ray upon the lush softness of her right breast. The girl gasped, writhed, turning her gorgeous dark eyes wildly in her pain and anguish.

"Shrew! Destroyer of men!" The young man's face contorted in primitive lust as the ray bored into the creamy whiteness o f o n e snowy mound. Straight through it cut, the little brown particles of dust seeming doubly incongruous disseminating from that source. Twice the brunette screamed. She grasped at her wounded body instinctively, and as rapidly jerked her hand away as the ray bit into it.

He was starting on the left breast when a man, beside himself with erotic frenzy, flung himself from the assembalge toward the scene of torture, crying: "I—I want to—"

Several others were affected by the man's contagious eagerness. They, too, leaped forward.

"I warned you!" snarled the man with the bigger instrument.

HE turned it on them, and the man with the pencil ray turned savagely to assist him. Terrible shrieks rent the air as the encroachers stopped short, turned and attempted to retreat. Again there was chaos as the inexorable

rays sublimated clothing to dust and disseminated human flesh. There was a mad scramble as the fear-crazed hordes attempted to flee. Women screamed, men shouted hoarsely as they fell or were pushed down, to be trampled.

Kirth Jonas was rather slight of build, and the fear-fury of the mob lifted him, flung him to the floor.

Someone kicked him in the head then, and everything began to blur. But with his last flicker of sight, he saw a panel open in a far wall, and a man step out of a noiseless elevator. There was something in the man's actions, in the way he looked at the crowd. . . .

And Kirth Jonas' ear, pressed against the floor, detected a strange vibration, a peculiar low humming sound which was *not* originating within his own head. . . .

He regained consciousness a few minutes later, to see first-aid attendants administering to the wounded prior to taking them away for more detailed medical attention. Aside from a headache, Jonas had suffered no injury. He arose unaided, but before he did that he noticed the vibration and the humming sound were no longer in evidence.

The two young men were apprehended while fleeing by a huge police paralysis-ray gun. They broke down sadly, cried like infants, and could not explain their actions.

Medical science, remarkably developed though it was, could find no clue. The young men were sane, normal. There was no trace of drugs in their bodies, or in the bodies of the others. So the matter remained for the time— a puzzle to all concerned.

But there *had* to be an explanation for the young men's actions, and for the similar actions of the others who had been in the thankorium that dreadful day, and one man finally had a clue.

"Marella," Kirth Jonas asked his

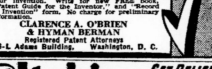
bride-to-be on the evening prior to the wedding, "do you still insist upon having the archaic ceremony in the thankorium?"

"Yes." She was a beautiful blonde girl, proud and haughty.

"Very well, then." Kirth Jonas sighed.

"I wonder just what you'd do if I were late?"

There was a good crowd of friends on hand at the wedding hour. It was not so good a crowd half an hour later. For the bridegroom, Kirth Jonas, had failed to put in an appearance. The bride, Marella, tapped her foot impatiently. Too low for them to hear, the vibration and the humming began below.

The guests were glowering at each other, looking for trouble, hoping for trouble—they were on the verge of another maelstrom of hate and berserk fury when—

A panel of the wall opened across the room, there was a sudden shout: "Restrain those impulses! Stop!" And Kirth Jonas stepped out of the noiseless elevator, tugging on the collar of a limp and nearly unconscious middle-aged fat man.

Hastily, Jonas raced across the room, clamped a wet and peculiar-smelling sponge over the nose of each of the angrier guests.

"There's a powerful soporific in that sponge," Jonas said. "The only soporific to make the human brain sluggish enough to protect it against the irascible and even murderous effects of—"

"What?"

"Well, essentially, to protect us from the several things science hasn't covered. Human hatred, jealousy, revenge. Science hasn't yet found a way to distill those things out of human nature. On the floor there by the elevator you see Beacon Terwillig." Jonas pointed. "He longed to be intimate with the pretty young girls who sing in the

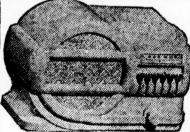

chorus here. None of them would succumb, including my Marella, though the Beacon made many furtive overtures. As you know, he is in his serious moments a great master of electrical research. For years he has conducted private investigations in the more outre aspects of the mysterious subject."

They stared at him, their anger subsiding with remarkable speed.

"Centuries ago," Jonas said, "the crude early scientists suspected that the *ions* in earth's atmosphere had a powerful by negative and irritating effect upon human conduct. When the earth passed through dense masses of these negative ions — electrically charged atoms—humans acted strangely, were prone to anger, short temper. Everything went wrong. But the subject was dropped, because science was too busy chasing more tangible rainbows, until these past few years."

"But what—"

"Beacon Terwillig, extraordinary scientist but sub-ordinary lover, discovered the secret of capturing, storing and discharging vast quantities of negative ions. In the sub-basement of this building he has, by dint of much labor and ingenuity, hidden a machine which discharges the ions over short areas in quantities ten times as great as the densest masses to be found in the air normally. Luckily for us all, I have a sensitive ear, and I detected the faint hum of his motors.

"We were made temporary savage beasts the other day," Jonas concluded, "and you were on the verge of becoming so again today. Hatred of the young girls he could not win, and the young man they favored, had become madness in the Beacon, and this was his consummate revenge.

"And no one would have known. The ion is a mighty electrical drug which leaves no trace of tangible clue. It is a sort of cosmic hashish."